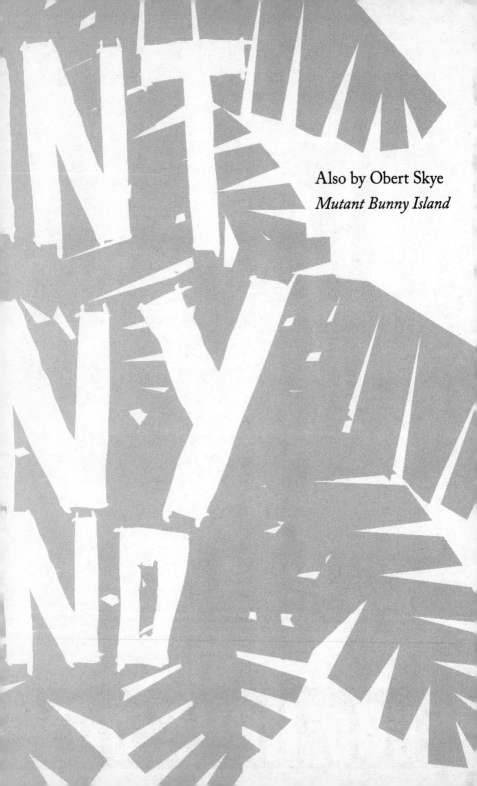

Also by Obert Skye
Mutant Bunny Island

MUTANT BUNNY ISLAND #2

BAD HARE DAY

BY OBERT SKYE

ILLUSTRATED BY EDUARDO VIEIRA

HARPER
An Imprint of HarperCollinsPublishers

Library of Congress Control Number: 2018933328
ISBN 978-0-06-239915-1

Typography by Joe Merkel
18 19 20 21 22 CG/LSCH 10 9 8 7 6 5 4 3 2 1
❖
First Edition

To my incredible sister, Julie,
who made sure our home was filled with animals
while growing up. Thanks for the memories and allergies.
—O.S.

To my parents, Ocelo and Eudete—thanks for the support
and patience. You're my all-time favorite heroes!
—E.V.

LASTERZOIDS
SQUID out of water!
2
EXTRA!!!
The James Prawn
MENACE!!!

CHAPTER ONE

BROUGHT BACK TO TALK SMACK

My whole body bounced as we drove away from the Bunny Island airport. My butt ached from sitting on the plane, and my throat was as thirsty as a squid in the desert. The air felt hot and smelled like the ocean mixed with perfume.

In front of the airport there were signs and banners advertising Carrot Con—the three-day festival that started this afternoon. It was set up to celebrate bunnies and the food they ate: the almighty, supposedly healthy, and completely disgusting carrot. I had been invited back to the island to be on a panel with my friends and talk about what had happened the last time I was here. We were going to have a few minutes to tell people about me

1

coming to the island to find my uncle, everyone being turned into mutant bunnies, and my friends and me saving everyone with some junk food.

We passed the big sign at the front of the airport. In the spirit of Carrot Con it had been temporarily changed to read: Bunny Island Hareport.

"It looks like everyone's excited for the Con!" I yelled.

"Superexcited, Perry," my uncle Zeke yelled back. "It's a big deal."

Zeke was driving me in a golf cart he had recently purchased. It was a four seater with a red base and white seats. He had painted a large purple squid on the top, and there were eight long foam tentacles hanging down from the roof. I held on to one of the tentacles as I sat in the front passenger seat and my uncle Zeke drove.

"So are you glad to be back, Perry?" he yelled as he swerved around hundreds of resting bunnies and then through some palm trees just south of the airport.

"Yes!" I yelled back as we bounced. "And a little sore."

I had wanted to return to Bunny Island since I had left it two months ago. I mean, Ohio was okay-o, and I liked my dad and all, but I missed the island and my friends here. When the Carrot Con committee had invited me to come back and be part of the festivities, I was beyond happy. Butt pain aside, I was glad to be back here. I looked at my uncle, and he smiled at me.

Zeke looked tan and in shape. He had on green shorts and a white T-shirt with an octopus on it. Beneath the octopus were the words *Suction Power*. And even though he looked like the spitting image of my father, his dark mustache and long brown hair made him appear much cooler than my dad.

"I'm just glad my dad let me come back so soon," I said happily.

"Me, too."

"I think he was sick of me moping around. Also, my allergies in Ohio were terrible. They don't seem to bother me here."

"That's strange."

"I know, it's like bunny fur makes me immune!"

Zeke swerved around a herd of bunnies that were resting in the shade of a large palm tree and crowding the narrow cobblestone road. Even though my uncle laid on the horn, the rabbits made no effort to move. They were confident that like the tourists on Bunny Island we wouldn't harm a single hair on these hares.

"When did you get this golf cart?"

"The Squidmobile? I bought it about a week after you left. I've made a few improvements to it since then."

"It's just like the vehicle Admiral Uli used in Issue #51: 'All Cods Go to Heaven.' The one where he couldn't get that warehouse fire put out on time. Those poor cods."

We bounced down the cobblestone path. I could see more banners hanging from some of the trees and big booths that were set up for Carrot Con. Ever since my friends and I stopped Mayor Lapin and his dastardly plot to turn everyone into rabbits, Bunny Island had become more popular than ever. The locals who had been turned into bunnies were semifamous. Everyone wanted to hear their stories and take pictures with them, and the island was trying to cash in on its newfound fame by holding the first-ever Carrot Con. People would be able to buy things like bunny ears and eat carrot cake and drink smoothies. Being turned into bunnies had been a horrible ordeal, but they were acting like it was all something exciting and fun. There were going to be bunny-themed talks and panels and even a huge color war where everyone was going to throw balls of colored orange dust at one another.

Part of the reason my dad had let me come back was because he knew I had played a key role in saving Bunny Island. Truth be told, I was kind of a hero. So, Dad knew that it was important I be here. He wanted to come with me, but unfortunately, due to his love of grains and growing things, he had some wheat-related meetings back in Ohio that he couldn't miss.

"By the way," Zeke said, "I like your new haircut."

"Thanks," I replied. "I cut it myself."

I reached up and touched my now spiky, blond hair. Two days ago, when I knew for sure that I was coming back, I had given myself a new look. I wanted to do something special for my return trip, so I had attempted to duplicate the hairstyle of Admiral Uli's starfish friend Barney. It didn't come out quite right, so I just put a lot of gel in it to make it stick up and hide any bald spots.

Blocking the path ahead of us was a group of at least fifty locals and "Bunny Mooner" tourists.

"What's happening?" I shouted to Zeke.

"I don't know," he replied as he stopped the Squidmobile behind the crowd. Everyone had their cameras out and were snapping shots of the trees toward the north. We hopped off the cart and weaseled our way through the people.

"Something tore up the forest," a lady with a large sun hat on told Zeke as he made his way to the front of the crowd.

I followed a step behind and was gobsmacked by what I saw. Even though this was only my second visit to the island, I knew the island well enough to know what certain parts should look like. And the part I was looking at now looked wrong. A row of trees was torn straight out of the ground, and the dirt was mounded like a snake made of soil.

"It was a storm or something," one overly tan lady

said. "Or maybe it has something to do with all this Carrot Con stuff."

"Did anyone see anything?" Zeke asked the crowd.

"I saw something," a short, sunburned man reported. "It tore across the path right in front of me. I was drinking a frozen smoothie, and I had to drop it so I could scream. Somebody owes me a new smoothie."

"That's not important. Do you know what it was?"

"Lime and toasted coconut."

"Not the flavor of your smoothie," Zeke said, frustrated. "The thing?"

"All I know is it was terrifying, like a small tornado, and now I'm smoothie-less."

The short man walked off as the crowd continued to swell. One of the island's police officers got out in front of the crowd and tried to keep the situation calm. His badge said Sheriff Rolly, and he had on green shorts and a green shirt and was uncomfortably tan. There was a whistle around his neck, and his head was completely bald.

"Nothing to see here," Rolly said. "Everyone go on. It's just some more strange weather. You all need to—" But his warnings were cut short when a small palm tree flew through the air in the distance. We all screamed as it slammed into the ground behind the sheriff. He flew forward, right into four women wearing identical orange T-shirts.

"Look!" Zeke hollered.

A big brown creature ripped through the trees in the distance, tossing up dirt and bushes in its wake as it moved away from us.

Now that we were reasonably safe, everybody began to *oooh* and *ahhh* and take pictures.

I looked at Zeke and he looked at me. Much like Admiral Uli communicated telepathically to his shrimp friends, I knew what my uncle was thinking. Thanks to *Ocean Blasterzoids*, we were pretty in sync. Sure, we could have stood around and screamed like the others, but as true squid cadets we were required to swim toward trouble.

Zeke took off after the mystery beast with me on his tail.

"I promised your dad I'd do a better job keeping you safe this time!" he yelled back at me as he ran.

"I won't tell if you don't."

It wasn't like me to be outside and running toward danger. Before my first visit to the island, I had been an indoor kind of squid, scared of just about every newt shadow I saw. But now, with what I had been through, it felt almost normal running after a strange creature not ten minutes after I'd landed.

It didn't take long for it to be obvious that the beast was way too fast for us to catch up to.

My uncle stopped running when we got to a small

stream. I was happy to do the same.

"That was incredible," Zeke said, remarkably not huffing and puffing at all.

"What was it?" I asked, doing enough huffing for the both of us.

"I'm not sure, but it's heading toward the west side of the island."

"It sure wasn't a tornado."

"Definitely not. But whatever it was it might explain a few things. Last week someone's house was torn apart and pushed into the ocean during the middle of the night. The week before that a huge sinkhole opened up under the library. The whole mystery section was swallowed up."

"You think that thing did it?"

"Might be fun to find out."

When we got back to the Squidmobile, the crowd was still there, looking confused and curious. Rolly was telling everyone to move on. He was also insisting that what we had just witnessed was just a freaky dust cloud. He ended his speech by reminding everyone to get their tickets for Carrot Con before it started in four hours.

"What do you think, Zeke?" he asked my uncle. "About that freaky dust cloud?"

"That was no cloud of dust."

"People's eyes can play tricks on them here on this

island," the sheriff said as if he was warning Zeke to keep quiet.

"My eyes are fine. And that was no trick," my uncle insisted as we climbed back into the Squidmobile.

"That makes it a mystery, then," I said.

Zeke smiled and nodded.

I love Bunny Island, and I was really excited to see my new best friend Juliet and get ready for the festivities, but to me it would be even better with a new mystery to solve. Uncle Zeke pulled away from the crowd and pressed down hard on the pedal. Instinctively, we both knew there was no time to waste.

CHAPTER TWO
UNDER AND OUT

A few blocks from Juliet's house, Zeke pulled the Squid-mobile over and turned it off. Hundreds of small bunnies began to circle around us as we sat parked.

"I have a surprise for you," Zeke said.

"Really?"

My uncle reached behind him and yanked up the backseat to access a compartment beneath it. He pulled out a small plastic box and then shut the seat. The box was purple and had a yellow *O* and *B* on the front of it.

"*Ocean Blasterzoids*," I whispered.

"I found these online. They might help us better communicate while you're here." He handed me the box, and I snapped open the plastic clasp and pulled the top off.

"Great floppy dorsal," I whispered excitedly.

I couldn't believe my eyes. In the box was a pair of Sharky-Barkys. They were a lot like walkie-talkies, but they came from the world of *Ocean Blasterzoids*. I had only seen them in the comics and had no idea they existed in real life. One was white and one was gray, but both of them were scaly looking and had dorsal fin antennas on top of them. On the front there was a shark-tooth-shaped knob that you could turn and a small speaker. There were two buttons on the sides and a small leather clip on the back of each of them.

I stared at them like they were long-lost treasure.

"Do they work?" I asked.

"Sure do." My uncle smiled. "They only made a few hundred of them a number of years ago. I've wanted a pair forever, and I thought I'd never find any."

He reached in the box and took out the gray Barky. I carefully retrieved the white one. We both clicked them on and a loud screech filled the air. All the bunnies that were gathered around the Squidmobile frantically hopped away.

"Perry, are you there?" my uncle said into his Sharky-Barky. "Under."

With normal walkie-talkies, you're supposed to say "over" when you're done speaking, but since Sharky-Barkys are typically used underwater, the correct thing to say is "under."

"I'm right here. Under."

We both smiled at each other. They worked perfectly. I felt like Admiral Uli having one in my hand.

Zeke turned the Squidmobile back on and drove me the rest of the way to Juliet's house.

"I'll wait right out here. If you need to talk to me, just hit me up on your Barky."

"I will."

"It's good to have you here, squid."

"It's better to be here."

I got off the Squidmobile and walked up to Juliet's house. Her home was small but well cared for. There were a lot of palm trees surrounding the front of her green house. The yard was filled with flowers of practically every color and home to about a billion bunnies.

I clipped the white Barky to my cargo shorts and walked to the front door. Juliet knew I was coming back, but she didn't know when. I brushed my hair up and stood as tall as I could. Then, with the confidence of Uli, I knocked on her door.

When she opened it, her green eyes went wide and her mouth opened to a size just under jumbo. I had never seen anyone so happy to see me.

"Perry!"

She threw her arms around me and jumped up and down while holding me tight. I tried to speak.

"I . . . can . . . you . . . so tight!"

Juliet let go so that I could breathe again.

"I can't believe you're here!" she exclaimed loudly. "This is perfect. Carrot Con is going to be amazing. We get to be on a panel together, and I'm going to compete in the Junior Miss Carrot contest. In fact, will you help me get ready?"

"I guess, but—"

"Thank you, Perry. You don't know how stressed I've been. The competition is pretty stiff."

"Actually, I—"

"I know, I know, I'm crazy to think I'll win, but my mom said that even if I fail I'll learn something. I just don't want to fail. Rain thinks I have a shot."

"Rain does?"

Juliet was so excited and she was talking superfast and loud. I kept trying to stop her, but she was like a game show contestant who'd just won the daily double.

"Hold on," I said, putting my hands up to shush her. "I'm sure you'll win the junior carrot thing, but there might be more important things going on."

Juliet looked confused. "Are you talking about your hair?"

"No. Why?" I asked. "I cut it myself."

"It looks, uh, awesome."

I would have felt really good about the compliment,

but Juliet had a backward sense of style. Having lived on the island her whole life, she didn't exactly have her finger on the pulse of what's totally geek and what's totally chic.

"Is that how everyone is doing their hair now in the States?"

"No, it's how certain starfish do."

Juliet smiled sincerely, and it reminded me how kind she really was.

"So, okay, what's this superimportant thing you want to talk about?"

"On the way over, we saw a a whole line of trees get torn up. Zeke thinks it's mysterious."

"Sounds like a little tornado? That's what you're freaking out about? That's nothing." Juliet seemed sad that it wasn't a mystery nearly as cool as our last adventure, when the mayor tried to turn everyone on the island into rabbits. "Microstorms have been messing up parts of the island for days."

"Really? I've never heard anyone talk about microstorms here before."

"Well, you weren't here for long. Now, come inside and help me work on my talent for the contest."

"What's your talent?"

"Ventriloquism."

"That's a talent?"

Juliet grabbed my right wrist and was attempting to

drag me into her house when my Sharky-Barky crackled to life.

"Perry, are you there? Under."

I took the white Barky off my pants and pressed the right button.

"Zeke, I'm here. Under."

"Just making sure these still work. Under."

"Okay. Under."

Juliet stared at me. "What are you doing? And what is that?"

"It's a Sharky-Barky. Zeke got them. They're pretty amazing."

"Are they squid related?"

"Yes. Admiral Uli uses them sometimes."

"It's nice to see you've grown up." Juliet was being funny, but it still stung a little. I had thought of her the whole time I was back in Ohio, and now she was already teasing me. Another golf cart came speeding up. It honked twice before skidding to a stop right next to the Squidmobile. A man I didn't recognize hopped out and handed Zeke an orange envelope. Then, as quickly as he had driven up, he sped off.

"Who was that?" I asked as Zeke tore open the letter and read it. He looked bewildered and unsettled. He smiled politely at Juliet and then glanced at me.

"We've been invited somewhere," he said while

thrusting the orange envelope in my direction.

I took it.

On the front it said:

READ IMMEDIATELY.

"What is it?" I asked.

"It's an invitation."

"From who?"

"Lady Beatrice."

Juliet gasped.

I did not.

CHAPTER THREE

NOT DELIGHTED TO BE INVITED

Lady Beatrice Hatch was one of Bunny Island's most prominent citizens. She was so prominent that I had never heard of her. Actually, I'm not sure what *prominent* really means; I think it mostly has to do with the fact that she is stinking rich. Zeke says she lives on the far west side of the island near the shut-down bunny sanctuary. She's a total recluse. She rarely comes into town, even though she owns half the island. But now for some reason she sent an invitation to my uncle asking him to bring me and my "companions" to her place for dinner. Apparently, she wanted to thank me for the help I had provided last time.

"How did she even know I was here?"

"She probably read in the *Daily Hare* that you were

coming to be a part of Carrot Con."

"Sure," Juliet said. "The paper said you'd be speaking with your friends. That's me."

I liked having Juliet call me her friend. My goal was to have her call me boyfriend by the end of my visit. Sure, she was almost eight months older than me, but every good squid deserves a special someone to be salty over.

"It's unusual for Lady Beatrice to invite anyone over," Zeke said. "Especially me. I used to work for her a long time ago, and we didn't end it on great terms."

"Don't we have a million better things to do?" I asked. "Don't you remember in *Ocean Blasterzoids* Issue #3 how Dr. Oily Cod invited those sardines over to his place and they ended up being made into salad dressing?"

"Of course. But Lady Beatrice is no Dr. Oily Cod. She and her husband, Owence, were the first people to bring bunnies over to the island. They tried to create a bunny paradise, but it didn't quite work how they planned." Zeke scratched his head. "Eventually, Furassic Park was shut down, and now all the bunnies that they brought over run wild."

"So she's to blame."

"Or thank."

"I think most people are happy the rabbits are here," Juliet said. "This would be just a normal, boring island without them."

"And now it's not normal at all." Zeke looked happy.

"Why would they care about meeting me?"

"There's no 'they,'" Zeke said. "Owence died years ago. She probably just wants some company and to thank you guys."

I sighed. "So it sounds like we're going to her house for dinner."

"I'd like to see the old place. Plus, Juliet and Rain can come."

"It might help my chances at the Junior Miss Carrot contest." Juliet looked almost as excited as when she had first seen me. "Lady Beatrice Hatch has some pull. And if I win, I get a five-hundred-dollar gift card."

"I'll tell you what," Zeke offered. "Let's get ahold of Rain and tell him what's happening. Then we'll all get dressed up and go out to the Hatch house tonight for dinner. At the very least, it's free food."

"And at the worst, it could be a trap."

Both Zeke and Juliet stared at me.

"A trap?" Zeke asked.

"Sure, a mysterious lady invites us all to dinner. It could end up inky."

"Let's take our chances." Zeke smiled to reassure me.

"Fine, but don't say I didn't warn you."

Juliet and I hopped onto the Squidmobile, and Zeke drove us to find Rain.

You made a big mistake.

And now all of oceankind will be **SCHOOLED** because of it.

CHAPTER FOUR

BAD SMELLS AND BAD FEELINGS

I had not come to Bunny Island to get dressed up. I had come to see Zeke and Juliet—and to a lesser extent Rain—and to participate in Carrot Con. I had not come to have dinner at a stuffy lady's house in the middle of the jungle. I didn't even have any nice clothes to wear. The best I could do was to put on my T-shirt that had a picture of Admiral Uli wearing a tuxedo on it. There was a speech bubble coming from his beak that said, "Dressed to krill." It was a quote from Issue #29 when Uli had to go undercover as a fancy Engfishman to take out a secret effusion of krill. *Effusion* is the snobby word krill call themselves as a group. Their uppity attitude was one of the reasons Uli had to take them out.

Now I was wearing my fancy T-shirt, and I had put on socks so my flip-flops looked more formal. Luckily, Rain didn't wear anything that much nicer, just a white T-shirt that said *Rain Train* and long shorts. In the beginning, the two of us had started off enemies, but now we tolerated each other. His bleached hair was shorter than before, and his dark skin and white teeth made him look like a celebrity. Rain was a few years older than me, but he didn't mind hanging around us because, as he put it, we were weird. The two of us even had a secret handshake that he had forgotten.

"Tentacles, tentacles, shark fin, shark fin, blowhole."

Rain and I sat in the backseat of the Squidmobile, and Juliet sat up front with Zeke. Zeke had put on a collared shirt for the occasion, and Juliet was wearing a denim skirt, and she looked prettier than I had ever seen her. I was going to tell her she looked as nice as the underwater eel moon of Coral Wicket, but I didn't have the courage.

"This is exciting," Zeke said.

"It is?" I questioned.

"Yes. We were going to just stay home and have spaghetti. Now we're having an experience."

"I like spaghetti," I pointed out.

"You'll like this better," he assured me.

"Is that how you do your hair now?" Rain asked as he looked at me. "Or is it just for tonight?"

My face burned red. I had been wondering if Rain would say anything about my new do.

"I cut it myself," I explained.

"I could have guessed that."

We drove through the town, out past the Bunny Bumps and the clearing, and into a dense part of the jungle I had never explored before. There was a thin dirt road that wound among thick palm trees and massive bushes. I couldn't see as many rabbits around, but I could hear the sound of strange birds, animals chirping and hollering. It was darker beneath the canopy of trees, and a spooky feeling spread over me like ink.

"I've never been out here," I said.

"Me neither," Juliet added.

"That's because no one is allowed on this part of the island," Rain informed us.

"It all belongs to Lady Beatrice Hatch and her husband," Zeke said. "They used to let others come out here about twenty years ago, when the sanctuary was open."

"Why did the sanctuary close?"

"Because Owence died." Zeke paused for effect. "There was an accident."

I couldn't stop my eyes from going wide. "What kind of accident?"

"Actually, it wasn't really an accident," Zeke said. "I just thought that sounded more exciting. He is dead, but the truth is people just stopped going since they could see plenty of rabbits for free all over the island."

The trees closed in and the forest floor grew even darker.

"This all still feels weird to me," Rain insisted. "Adults never want to just thank kids for anything."

"Rain's right." I leaned forward in my seat to look at my uncle as he drove. "My dad thanked me last week for not wiping my mouth on the tablecloth, but then when I wiped it on the curtains instead, he went all nuts."

"Exactly," Rain said.

"It's not a trick." My uncle seemed excited. "It's an honor."

"You sound like you actually want to go to this," I said, confused.

"Nobody really gets to see her anymore. She's like the Willy Wonka of bunnies."

"That would make sense if she raised chocolate bunnies," Rain said, sounding as disappointed as I felt. "But she doesn't."

"At least we get to go together," Juliet said in an attempt to make things seem better. "And this will help her to know who I am when she's judging the Junior Miss Carrot contest."

"You really want to win, don't you?" I asked.

"A little, I guess. Okay, a lot."

"I get it. We'll sacrifice for you. But something about it all still feels slimy to me."

"It'll be okay," my uncle assured me. "It's just dinner. Really what could go wrong?"

"That's exactly what Uli said right before he was attacked by those invisible newts."

The forest got thicker and the night grew dimmer. Birds stopped chirping, and just when it seemed like the vegetation was about to close around us completely, the Squidmobile rolled out onto a wide brick driveway.

And I breathed again.

The path led to a house big enough to be a small hotel. It was three stories tall and painted a dull shade of yellow. There were vines and bushes growing all over it and a clay tiled roof that was faded from sun and time. In front of the house was a large lawn and a fountain shaped like a bunny with wings for ears. All over the lawn I saw small ceramic bunny gnomes in various poses and colors.

"Wow," Juliet said. "It's beautiful."

"I guess," Rain said. "It looks overgrown."

Zeke pulled the Squidmobile around the fountain and up to the front door.

"I don't want to sound like a coward," I told them all, "but this seems like the kind of place where newts would live, or people would go before they turn up missing."

Zeke got out and the three of us followed him up six

wide stone steps that led to a large front door shaped like a big rabbit head. He knocked on the nose, and the loud hollow sound made all of us shiver. As I looked around, I noticed that there were no real bunnies on the lawn, or anywhere, for that matter.

"Hey, where are the bunnies?" I asked.

All of us glanced around.

"Weird," Rain said. "Lady Beatrice is the bunny woman. Her place should be swimming in them."

"And do we have to call her *lady*?" I asked. "I don't get that. Is it just something people do at her home? Am I 'Man Perry' here?"

"More like 'Boy Perry,'" Rain suggested.

Before I could protest or get a real answer the door opened, and I immediately recognized the man who opened it as the guy who had delivered the invitation. He was wearing a blue suit and yellow tie now, but he had the same old, squinty eyes.

"I am Bouncer. Please come in."

His words sounded like a long, slow burp.

"No, thank you," I said as the hair on the back of my neck stood up.

"Hello, Bouncer," my uncle said. "Actually, what Perry meant to say is, we'd love to come in."

"Actually," I insisted, "what I meant to say was—"

Zeke shut me up by pushing me into the house. Juliet

and Rain didn't need to be shoved. For some reason, they followed my uncle in without hesitating.

The house was decorated with huge, leafy potted plants and bunny-patterned wallpaper. I touched the edge of a small table and realized there was dust everywhere. If Bouncer was a servant, he wasn't doing a very good job of keeping the place clean. The floors were ornate marble, and the windows were all cloudy, allowing only weak light to come in. The thing that stood out to me the most was the smell. It smelled like someone had been cooking broccoli in latex paint.

"Do you sort of feel like you're walking into a trap?" I said.

Juliet didn't reply.

CHAPTER FIVE

FURASSIC PARK

Bouncer stopped by a large coatrack and asked if he could take our jackets. Since none of us were wearing jackets, I think he was probably being sarcastic.

"I have been instructed to take you to the sanctuary before dinner," Bouncer informed us. "So if you will follow me to the tram."

"There's a tram?" Zeke asked.

"It was put in right after you were . . . let go."

"That's a nice way of saying it."

"I wasn't trying to be nice," Bouncer said dryly.

We followed Bouncer through the house. He led us down a long hallway and through a dozen rooms before we arrived at a large glass conservatory at the back of the house.

Sitting inside the conservatory was a big red-and-blue tram car that was about ten feet long and four feet wide. We could see the tram tracks leading off into the dark of the forest.

"Will Lady Beatrice be joining us for the trip?" Zeke asked.

"No" was all Bouncer said.

We climbed into the tram. There were eight hard wooden chairs, and the cart had windows on all sides so that we could see out in every direction. Bouncer went to the front of the cart and took the driver's seat. There were two red buttons on a small podium next to a brass lever.

Bouncer pushed one of the red buttons, and the tram began to shake and hiss. He threw the brass lever forward, and we all lurched back into our seats.

Slowly, the tram began to move out of the conservatory and away from the house and into the thick trees.

"I thought we were just having dinner?" Juliet said.

"This is better than dinner," I replied, suddenly happy to be away from the smell and heading somewhere mysterious on a mysterious contraption.

The tram ran on a thin track similar to a train. There was no train engine, just a thick wire in front pulling us forward and through the jungle. There was also a wire on the back that was hopefully going to pull us back after dinner.

"How long is this ride?" I asked.

"You'll see."

"Will we still get to meet Lady Beatrice?" Juliet asked. She bit her bottom lip, looking concerned.

Bouncer sighed. "Unless something drastic happens."

"That's concerning," Rain said. "It seems like ever since I met Perry everything's been drastic."

"Squids love drama," I pointed out.

"Does Lady Beatrice have any children?" Juliet asked.

A vein on Bouncer's forehead throbbed.

"No more questions," he said.

As the tram trundled up a small hill, Bouncer began to sing a strange song. His deep, burpy voice and odd manner of speech made the song uncomfortable to listen to.

"They will hop into your heart from the very, very start.
They will win your love and favor by and by.
For a bunny is a friend and a friend until the end,
And they'll be with all of us until we die."

We shivered as a group.

And then even though none of us was exactly asking for an encore, he started into another song.

"If by chance you meet a bunny, do not let it go.
For every bunny that you capture has four feet, you know.
Those lucky feet are worth a bundle, worth a coin or two,
So chop them off and make a wish—you'll be glad you do."

34

"That one's even worse than the first one," I told Bouncer.

He looked hurt. "I don't get a chance to sing for many people these days. Years ago, I would take visitors out to Furassic Park all the time. The guests always loved my songs."

"They might have been lying," I informed him. "Or maybe back then people had worse taste in music."

Zeke nudged me. "What my nephew is trying to say is that perhaps you should just whistle."

Bouncer began to whistle.

"You know, salamanders and newts live in jungles," I informed the three people who weren't whistling.

"I'm well aware of that," Zeke said.

"Can we promise no newt talk at dinner?" Juliet scrunched her face up. "We're going to have dinner with one of the most influential people on the island. Do you think I'll have a chance to give her a preview of my Junior Miss Carrot talent?"

"What is your talent?" Rain asked.

"Ventriloquism."

"Maybe save that for another time," I suggested.

"Okay," Juliet said with her mouth partly closed and trying to make it look like it wasn't her talking.

The tram cart moved out from under the trees into a large clearing where there was a tall wooden wall covered with vines and green growth. In the middle of the wall were two massive gates that swung open as the tram moved through. Above the gate was a weather-worn sign that read:

FURASSIC PARK

"Clamtastic," I whispered.

"How big is this place?" Juliet asked Zeke.

"It takes up the whole west end of the island."

The tram went over a wide river and through the gates, where it passed over another moat. Everywhere I looked I could see deep green grass. Inside the wall, there were large wire cages with wooden frames. There were abandoned buildings and old vehicles that were so overgrown they were practically part of the forest. The hills in the distance were connected with large tubes, like an enormous hamster city.

"All this for bunnies?" I asked Zeke.

Bouncer overheard and decided to answer.

"All of this for mankind. Bunnies are essential to life."

"Is that true?" Rain questioned him. "I mean, they're cute and all, but essential to life?"

Bouncer looked hurt. "Imagine your existence without them."

"Okay." Rain closed his eyes and took a moment to

imagine. "Not much different."

Bouncer looked bothered, and his eyes were squintier than ever.

As the tram clicked along the track, I felt more and more uncomfortable. The mist brushed past like it had fingers. The windows clotted with moisture.

The tram eased into a big, abandoned tram station and shuddered to a stop near a large wooden platform. I made a move to get out, but the tram door was locked.

"No," Bouncer said firmly. "We won't be getting out."

"Why?"

"It's not wise."

I rubbed the water off the window and peered out through the circle I'd made. I could see that the station was completely dilapidated. The platform was splintered and falling apart. The ticket booth looked like someone had taken a hammer to all its windows. The stairs that led down were weed-covered and rickety looking.

"Can we just look around a little?" Zeke asked. "I promise we won't touch anything."

"No!" Bouncer was serious. "I'm not worried about you touching things. Let's just say that ever since the sanctuary closed, the rabbits in here have taken on a passive-aggressive nature. Emphasis on *aggressive*. They don't come out unless they are bothered or hungry. Sometimes they tolerate humans; sometimes they don't. It's best to leave them be."

"Should we even be here?" Juliet asked.

"Who's to say?" Bouncer said. "Of course, Lady Beatrice wouldn't have had me bring you out if it were truly dangerous. Besides, I have a net gun on board. If any rabbits get out of hand, I can corral them with that."

"A net gun?" I said excitedly. "Admiral Uli's sister, Julie, has a wet blanket gun. She can shoot it on anything to ruin the fun."

Bouncer stared at me for a long moment before he continued talking.

"Anyway, Lady Beatrice just thought it would be a treat for you all to see this old place. It's a spot most people will never see. Furassic Park now belongs to the rabbits. We should return to the house. Dinner should be ready shortly."

"I remember it being much nicer," Zeke said. "It was so alive before; now it seems dead."

"Oh, I assure you it very much isn't."

Bouncer turned the tram back on and then pulled the lever back so we would move in the reverse direction we had come. When the cart didn't move, he wiggled the lever back and forth a few times. When that did nothing, he cursed and then turned the engine off.

"Please excuse my language and the delay," he apologized. "If you'll all just remain seated."

Bouncer got up and opened the door.

"Should you bring your net gun?" I asked.

"That won't be necessary," he replied.

Bouncer stepped out of the tram cart and walked to the front of it, where he opened up a large panel and began to tinker with something.

"This is weird, right?" Juliet asked.

"I think so," I answered her. "If I didn't know any better, I'd say Bouncer was a Newt."

"I don't think you know any better," Rain pointed out. "He's just a weird butler who has hair growing out of his ears."

"It wasn't that long ago when you were half bunny and had hairy ears growing out of your head," I reminded Rain.

Rain touched the top of his head and didn't say anything.

"I do wish he'd let us walk around." Zeke was busy looking out the windows as he spoke. "I'd love to explore it now. It looks so different from the last time I saw it."

"It reminds me of the sharktuary," I said. "The one in the special-edition *Ocean Blasterzoids: Humpback of No Return*. What was that whale's name?"

"Humpty Wumpty," Zeke said.

Rain shook his head. "You two should get out more."

"I'm going to see if Bouncer needs help," my uncle said as he opened the door and stepped out.

"I'm coming with you," I said, hurrying out after him.

I thought Juliet and Rain would follow me, but they didn't. I stood next to my uncle as he stood next to Bouncer as Bouncer messed with some wires on the front of the tram.

"Can you see the problem?" Zeke asked.

I thought my uncle was making a joke about how squinty Bouncer's eyes were, but if he was, Bouncer didn't get it.

"I do see the problem," he said. "Occasionally, bunnies get into the wiring and chew through things. I'll have it fixed in a second. You two should get back inside."

"It seems safe enough out here," I pointed out.

"Things aren't always what they seem." Bouncer twisted two wires together. "Now, if you'll get back inside, I'm almost—"

Bouncer stopped talking, and I could hear the faint sound of something clicking.

"Is that the tram?" I asked.

"No," Bouncer said. "Get inside the cart—quickly."

The clicking grew louder, and it was now followed by the sound of something pounding.

It was Zeke's turn to ask a question. "What is that?"

I turned to look and I couldn't believe my eyes. At the edge of the wooden platform were thousands of bunnies. They were beating their feet against the ground and clicking their teeth.

"Get in!" Bouncer insisted.

Juliet pulled open the door and all three of us pushed in. Rain was standing in the tram looking out at the rabbits.

"There's so many," he said.

"That's true. And since they rarely see people, they can be a bit overly affectionate." Bouncer moved to the controls and started the tram. It came to life, but when he pulled the lever back nothing happened. "Whiskers," he cursed. "We need to give it a push start. A few good shoves should kick it into action and get the cables pulling us back home."

"I'll do it," Zeke volunteered.

"It'll take all four of you," Bouncer said with authority. "I'd help, but I have a bad back. Hurry."

As he spoke, I saw him smile ever so slightly.

Before I could say anything, we all piled out of the tram as quickly as we could, leaving Bouncer inside with the door open. The four of us jumped onto the tracks at the front of the tram and tried to push it in the direction we had come. But it was too heavy. We couldn't get it to move.

"Harder!" Zeke said.

We groaned and pushed again.

"The rabbits!" Juliet yelled.

I looked away from the tram and saw the mass of rabbits drawing closer, their chattering and thumping growing louder and louder by the moment.

"Push!" I hollered.

The tram lurched forward and began to move down the tracks inch by inch, but the engine still wouldn't start.

We moaned and struggled and pushed with all our might.

The thumping and chattering were now joined by the sound of chirping. I've never known rabbits to chirp, but that's what they were doing. They were staring at us with their thousands of adorable, angry faces, and chirping.

We pushed again as hard as we could.

The rabbits stopped thumping then and began to slowly jump toward us.

"It's rolling," Zeke said. "Get in!"

We all stopped pushing and ran for the door. Rain, Juliet, and Uncle Zeke made it in without a problem, but I tripped and fell to the ground, landing on my face in the gravel next to the track.

"Perry!" Juliet screamed.

I pulled myself up and ran as fast as I could. The rabbits' thumping became thunderous. The tram engine finally kicked in, and the cart started moving away quickly.

"Faster!" Zeke commanded as he held his arm out of the open door for me to grab.

"I'm not a good runner!" I yelled back.

"Just take my hand!"

I grabbed for my uncle's hand and missed. I stumbled and fell to the ground again. The rabbits were now right behind me. Zeke jumped out of the tram and ran back to help me. He picked me up and pushed me forward.

"Run, Perry! Run!"

The tram had seemed to be so slow-moving when we had come, but now it seemed like a rocket. Zeke pushed me as he ran behind. When it became clear that we weren't going to make it, he picked me up and ran with me under his arm like I was a football. He heaved me in through the open door and jumped in behind me a split second later. Juliet slid the tram cart door shut mere moments before the bunnies smashed against it. Wave after wave of rabbits finally reached us and crashed up over the cart and against the sides. The glass was too slippery for them to hold on to, so the bunnies would hit and then slide slowly to the ground as we made our getaway.

I fell onto the floor of the tram between the seats, exhausted and well aware that things like this never happened to me back in Ohio.

"I thought we were going to be smothered," Zeke said.

"You really aren't a strong runner, are you, Perry?" Rain observed.

"I'm better at skipping, remember?" I answered

honestly. "What's up with those rabbits?"

"I'm not the one to ask," Zeke said.

We all turned our heads to look at Bouncer.

"They are uneasy these days," he said. "I suppose being studied and experimented on for years has made them a bit hoppy. Who knows how they will act from one day to the next?"

The tram rolled over the moat and out through the gates. I was happy to leave Furassic Park behind us, but my tentacles were tingling. Something about the experience seemed odd and almost set up.

"Why did you take us there?" I asked Bouncer. "We almost got killed!"

"Beatrice asked me to. It's not my fault the tram stopped working. Most of her visitors love seeing the place. And besides, those rabbits wouldn't have killed you," Bouncer said, trying to calm me down. "They might have scratched and bitten, but unless they somehow decided to all work together to suffocate you, you would have been fine. Now, let's get you all to the house. Dinner should be just about ready."

Bouncer made me uneasy. Like an honest newt, or a clever salamander, something about him did not seem right.

OCEAN BLASTERZOIDS

SQUID OUT OF WATER

CHAPTER SIX

DISGUSTING IS SERVED

When we got back to the house, Bouncer led us to a large dining room with a remarkable stained glass window of a rabbit on one end, pink bunny wallpaper on the other walls, and purple carpeting. It hurt my eyes just to be in the room. In the center of the space, there was an enormous table with plates and glasses on it. Bouncer pulled out a chair for Juliet to sit down. I waited for him to help me, but it never happened. So I pulled out my own seat and sat down next to Juliet and Rain. Zeke sat across the table so that all three of us were staring at him.

"Lady Beatrice will be with you shortly," Bouncer burped.

As soon as he was out of the room, we all began to talk

and chatter about how strange the Furassic Park sanctuary had been and how much Bouncer creeped us out.

"I think he wanted us to get attacked," I whispered. "I saw him smile. He was just pretending the tram didn't work so we'd get outside of it."

"I don't think that's true," Zeke said. "I don't think he's capable of smiling. Besides, he wanted us to stay in the tram at first."

It wasn't like my uncle to not be suspicious. I stared at him, wondering if he was okay.

"What?" he said. "I think Bouncer's okay."

"I don't think the bunnies would have hurt us anyway," Juliet added. "They weren't mutant like the ones we dealt with last time."

"Still . . ." I started to say.

"Still, I bet you're going to make a big deal out of it," Rain said nicely. "You always do. Maybe it was some crab or turtle thing you like."

"I like squids."

"Whatever," Rain added.

"Let's just have a nice dinner and be honored that we were invited," Zeke suggested.

"Dinners can be deadly," I insisted. "This meal invitation reminds me of the time when Admiral Uli was invited to dinner at the Halibut House and then nearly got steamed by a knot of naughty newts."

"See, you're good at making a big deal of things," Rain pointed out. "And talking junk."

"What if she serves us bunny?" I asked.

I gasped at my own words. I hadn't thought about the fact that Beatrice Hatch would be feeding us anything until right at that moment. Not all food was my friend. In fact, if it wasn't covered in sugar and fried, I didn't spend much time with it. Looking around at the stuffy, overgrown house, I could only imagine the old and disgusting things she might make me eat. Creamed liver? Boiled brain? Salads?

I shivered.

"She's not going to serve bunny." Juliet scoffed at me. "She likes rabbits, remember? Plus, she's rich, so the food will probably be good."

"But . . ." Rain sniffed. "If that smell is coming from whatever she's cooking, I can tell it's not going to be good."

A door opened on the far side of the dining room and Bouncer came out, followed by an old woman. He stopped and motioned toward her with his hands.

"Lady Beatrice Hatch," he announced.

It sounded like he wanted us to clap, so I did. We all stood up, but nobody else clapped, so I stopped. Rain politely laughed at me, and Juliet looked embarrassed.

"Sorry," I whispered.

Lady Beatrice stepped all the way into the dining

room. She had on a heavy yellow dress that made her look like a large cob of lumpy corn. She had stringy, orange hair and a nose so big that it would make a porpoise jealous. She walked to a chair a few spots away from Zeke, and Bouncer pulled her seat out.

I don't know how else to say it, but when she sat down, she farted.

Juliet looked at me and I looked at her. We both looked at Rain and then glanced at Zeke, wondering what to do. I wanted to laugh, but I was pretty sure that wasn't proper etiquette. I know that breaking wind is a part of life; I just have a difficult time not cracking up about it. Admiral Uli also has a weak spot for bathroom humor. Of course, in *Ocean Blasterzoids* they call it bubbling, not farting.

Bouncer helped Lady Beatrice scoot in and she bubbled again.

We all kept standing because that seemed like good manners even though Mrs. Beatrice herself had just double bubbled. I put my hand over my mouth to keep from laughing.

"Hello, Lady Beatrice," Zeke said respectfully. "It's been a long time, but you look lovely."

I had never heard my uncle lie before.

"Mr. Owens," she replied. "It has been a while. Please have a seat."

Zeke sat down, and I kept standing with my friends.

She turned her head and hair to look at me and my friends. "And you are?"

"I'm Juliet."

"I'm Rain."

"And I'm Perry."

"Yes, the three children who saved the day."

We all just stood there looking as uncomfortable as fish in a hot pan.

"Such bravery." Another bubble. "Taking on Mayor Lapin like that. You've brought a lot of attention to this island. Some good, some bad."

"Sorry about the bad parts," I apologized.

"Me, too. You may be seated," she told us.

We all sat down as she continued to talk.

"Perry, when I heard you were returning to the island I knew I needed to meet you—immediately. I didn't get the chance to meet you kids when you were here before. I was away on business. And I certainly didn't want to miss the opportunity this time. I needed to take a long look at you all." She stared at all of us slowly, her eyes finally resting on me. "You're here to attend this ugly Carrot Convention?"

Something didn't feel right. Lady Beatrice was giving me the shrimps. I looked at Zeke to see if maybe he wanted to just make a run for it with me. Beatrice seemed horrible, and she was a bubbler, and the way she talked reminded me of Clam-ity Jane, the first female villain Uli ever tangled with. She was a rich, stubborn clam who had tricked Uli into giving away the location of his hideout by making him take a pearlygraph test. I didn't like the way Beatrice looked, and her voice made my squid skin shiver.

"You're here for the convention?" she asked again, still waiting for my answer. "What's the matter, Perry? Bunny got your tail?"

I cleared my throat. "Yes, I came for Carrot Con. We're doing a panel on the last day. I also came early to spend time with my friends first."

"Ah, friendship, such a lovely thing." She turned her attention to Rain. "Rain, I believe I know your mother, Flower."

"I think you do."

"I know I do. I was just being polite. She runs that little juice shack that helped serve all those smoothies."

Rain nodded.

"And Juliet, I think your father works at one of my hotels in town."

"He does."

"Again, just being polite. No need for you to reply. And Zeke, you haven't been out to see me in ages."

"I didn't think I was welcome anymore."

"Perhaps you aren't, but I'm curious about what I hear. You were a bunny for a spell. How envious I am."

Lady Beatrice bubbled.

"It wasn't a good thing," my uncle informed her.

"Well, I'm not sure I agree. I think I'd rather enjoy being a bunny. Such wonderful creatures. Wouldn't you agree, Perry?"

I wasn't sure why she was asking me, but I nodded.

"You all saw the sanctuary?"

"A little of it," Zeke said.

"Well, it is quite vast. I'm glad you got a peek. There are miles of tunnels and hutches. Such a beautiful place. Such a pity it had to close. You can't keep funding something nobody visits. But enough about sad things. Let's eat."

Beatrice picked up a small golden bell that was sitting on the table near her right hand and rang it loudly. All of us plugged our ears.

A door on the other side of the dining room opened and maids came out of the kitchen carrying gold trays with silver domes on them. They set the trays on the far end of the table and began to serve us all. The plates they put in front of us had silver domes over them so that we couldn't see what they were.

I pulled off the silver dome and almost passed out. It was just as I feared: there, sitting in front of me, was a salad. Not a Jell-O salad, or pudding salad, or even potato salad. It was a pile of leaves and twigs and some carrot shavings. I looked across the table at Zeke and pleaded with my eyes for him to somehow put a stop to this nonsense. He just looked back at me helplessly.

"The dressing is in the small bottles near your plates," Beatrice informed us. "It's a fig-and-lavender syrup."

My head was getting light.

"I find a good salad makes me feel right with the world. The bunnies we all love so well know how to eat properly. This dish is inspired by them. Tell me, Zeke, what did you eat while in your bunny condition?"

Zeke was poking at his salad with his fork, looking almost as disappointed as me.

"We ate a lot of purple carrots," he answered. "But they tasted like pizza and chips."

"Well, I believe you'll find this salad to be equally delicious. The field greens are so fresh you can still taste the dirt on them."

My will to live began to shrivel.

I looked at my friends and was shocked to see that Juliet and Rain were actually eating their salads. They didn't look happy about it, but they were being polite and putting forkfuls of green in their mouths. Zeke also took a bite of his. I refused to give in, so I moved the grassy food around on my plate to make it look like I had eaten some.

"Tell me, Perry." Beatrice acted like polite society, but

she was talking with her mouth full and bubbling. "How did you ever come to find an antidote for your uncle's bunny condition?"

"It was an accident, really."

"How interesting." A small fleck of lettuce flew out of her mouth and landed on the other end of the table. "It's amazing how accidents can save the day. Of course, in my day children didn't go about saving the world. They kept to themselves and let the adults worry about such matters."

I was confused. "So I shouldn't have saved my uncle? Someone had to do it."

"And someone did," she said, followed by a long sniff. "Of course, we have a police force on the island. My nephew, Rolly, is the sheriff. I'm sure he had things well in hand."

"I don't think he did," I told her.

Zeke looked at me as if I was being rude.

Lady Beatrice wiped her pale face with a napkin. "You're an outsider, Perry," she said in the most patronizing way she could. "You don't understand that we locals have certain ways to handle things. Your friends are locals. They understand. You're just lucky that all's well that ends well. You saved the day, and we will be grateful."

It didn't sound like she was grateful, but I was happy to have the conversation end.

"Now"—Lady Beatrice clapped—"the meal continues."

CHAPTER SEVEN
HARENAPPED

Beatrice rang the bell again and the servants returned. They mercifully took our salad plates and then vanished into the kitchen.

"A small bit of green salad helps with digestion." Beatrice bubbled. "It also prepares the palate for the main course. You should all take a moment to wipe your faces."

There was nothing on any of our faces, but we all picked up our napkins and took a good swipe. I was relieved that the first part of dinner was over, but worried about what was coming next.

"Before the main course comes out, I thought I should tell you both something," Beatrice said.

"Both?" I asked, knowing that she had four guests.

"Juliet and Rain can listen, but I think this will mean more to you and your uncle than to them. You see, I've done a little research. You're sort of famous here, Perry. You found the antidote. Because of that I want to know all about you."

"What sort of research have you done?" Zeke asked, sounding confused.

"I like to know who's coming to dinner. For example, I didn't know that you and Rain's mom, Flower, were seeing each other."

"We're trying to keep that a secret," Zeke said.

"Whoops, the secret's out. Also, I was fascinated to learn that Perry brought junk food here when he first came. According to island law, that's illegal."

"That junk food helped save us all," I reminded her.

"Don't worry. Please keep calm. I'm not going to turn Perry in. I just wanted you to know that I know how to find things out."

"I thought this was a friendly visit." Zeke seemed upset.

"Oh, it is friendly," Lady Beatrice insisted. "It's just that I take the activity of this island very seriously. When my husband and I first brought bunnies here, it was with the desire to make it a haven of sorts. A place where they would be free to hop and live. Now Perry has saved us all, and I need to make sure he's the kind of person I want representing our island."

"I'm not representing anything," I insisted. "I just wanted to save my uncle from being a rabbit forever."

"How sweet. Let's not talk about this any longer."

She stared at me and then rang the bell again.

The doors opened and once more the servants were coming in with trays. They set them on the table and then divvied them out to all of us. Our plates were covered with silver domes again. I left mine covered until Beatrice gave us permission to remove the lid. I pulled off the cover, and there sitting in front of me was a sight worse than salad. It was gray and charred and it reminded me of . . .

"Wait . . ." I pushed myself away from the table. "What is this?"

Beatrice smiled. "Why, it's squid, of course."

I didn't want to scream, but I did. It was a long, loud, terrifying yelp. Lady Whoever said she had done her research. Now here she had slaughtered some squids and placed them on our plates. It had to mean something. She was working with newts, or she was part of some evil plan to put an end to squids everywhere.

"What's the matter, Perry?" she asked. "Squid is quite the delicacy. Once you taste it, you'll be hooked."

I stood up and dropped my napkin on my plate. I wanted to cover the poor squid who had given its life to help Beatrice make her sick, twisted point.

"This isn't right," I said. "We should go."

"Why?" Beatrice asked. "Is the squid not cooked to your liking?"

Zeke looked at me and then motioned for me to sit down. I couldn't believe he wasn't as outraged as I was. There was a dead squid on my plate, and someone needed to pay for it. Lady Butt Face must have found out that we were fans of Admiral Uli and then found one of his compadres to fry up.

There was no way I was going to eat it. I thought it might be a good idea to point at Beatrice and call her evil, but my thoughts were interrupted by the stained glass window breaking due to a giant whirling cyclone of fur that broke through it and tore into the room. Amid the whirling and spinning, I could see that it was a gigantic bunny that swooped in.

Our hostess screamed, and I flew back into my chair and onto my butt.

The beast lifted Beatrice up and wrapped its arms around her. As it was grabbing her, I could see that it was a massive brown rabbit with ears the size of ironing boards and a body as large as a car. It had red eyes and a collar of some sort around its neck. The animal screeched and whipped its whiskers around, cutting me on the right cheek and Juliet above her left eye.

"Help!" Beatrice screamed.

Bouncer and the other servants came running into the dining room. One of the servants fainted when she saw the rabbit. Another began to pray. Bouncer picked up a broom and began swinging at the monster. I grabbed my fork and tried to stab it.

But the massive rabbit threw Beatrice over its shoulder and then it bounded back out of the broken window and into the trees outside.

"Stop that beast!" Bouncer screamed.

Zeke ran to the window and climbed outside, but it was too late. The massive bunny and Lady Beatrice were long gone.

CHAPTER EIGHT

SAVED BY THE TAIL

Juliet, Rain, and I caught up to my uncle, who had run out the shattered window.

"Do you think that's the same rabbit that tore down those trees earlier?"

"I hope so," Zeke replied. "Because I don't want to think about what it means if there's more than one."

"Should we chase after it?" Rain asked.

"It's just a *giant* bunny," Juliet pointed out. "A giant bunny that picked up a full-grown woman and carried her off."

I looked at all of them. "I feel bad, but she did serve us squid."

"It doesn't matter if she served us squid or if she stole

anything in the past and fired me when I caught her, we have to help her," Zeke insisted. "To the Squidmobile!"

"I'm just happy I don't have to eat any more of her food."

Everyone stared at me.

"And sad that she was harenapped," I added.

We ran as fast as we could to the Squidmobile and hopped in like we were part of an action movie. But instead of tearing off, Zeke fumbled around, looking for something on the floor.

"Where are the keys?" he asked. "I know I left them in the ignition," he said.

"Maybe Bouncer knows where they are," I suggested. "Or maybe they have a car we can use."

"Good thinking," Zeke said. "Well, not good thinking, but adequate thinking."

Zeke jumped out of the Squidmobile and ran back up the steps and into the house while Rain, Juliet, and I waited in the cart.

"How come whenever you come here, things get nuts?" Rain said. "It was so nice and peaceful while you were gone."

"That's true," Juliet said. "You're here one afternoon and stuff is already crazy. Don't get me wrong, I'm glad you're back, but just once, I'd like it to be for a normal visit."

"You and me both," I said. "Normal would be nice."

"You two are way past normal," Rain said. "Even

small things get big and weird with you around."

"Like that rabbit. It was huge," Juliet said. "Way bigger than anything I've seen before."

"And it just picked her up," Rain said sounding a little impressed.

"I know," I said. "I was wishing she would go away, but I didn't mean like that."

Zeke ran back then, huffing like he'd been sprinting the whole way.

"Bouncer is inside mumbling and not making any sense. But one of the cooks said that the large bunny had been spotted earlier in the week out by the swimming pool."

"Why didn't they tell anyone?" I asked.

"Beatrice was afraid someone would hunt it. They think it lives somewhere in the sanctuary."

Juliet's face scrunched up. "If they thought there was a giant rabbit out there, then why did they have us visit the place?"

Zeke looked at me. "Perry, are you thinking what I'm thinking?"

"Someone should invent hand shoes?" I answered honestly.

"No." Zeke shook his head. "I think we should pay another visit to Furassic Park."

Juliet shivered as Rain pretended not to. Me? I put

aside thoughts of hand shoes and tried to look half as brave as my uncle.

Before we could turn to walk toward the tram, we were stopped in our tracks by Bouncer. He was holding a large machete and squinting at us.

"Not so fast," he said. "You're not going anywhere. Lady Beatrice is missing, and it looks like you're to blame."

"What are you talking about?" Zeke asked. "That makes no sense."

"It is the only explanation I can think of." Bouncer continued to hold the enormous knife. "So I have summoned the law. The police are on the way."

I was going to say something, but my words were halted by the faint sound of an approaching police siren.

OCEAN BLASTERZOIDS
SQUID OUT OF WATER

CHAPTER NINE

FRAME GAME

I don't know how the police had gotten to Lady Beatrice's so fast. It had only been a few minutes since the ladynapping, and already there was a cop coming straight toward the house. The only way anyone could have arrived so soon was if they had been driving in the jungle nearby when Bouncer called.

Bouncer held the machete like it was his duty and insisted we not move. The cop golf cart had red and blue lights on it and was painted blue. At the wheel was Sheriff Rolly, Lady Beatrice's nephew. He pulled up to the house and got out of his vehicle.

"What's going on?" Rolly asked. "I should be helping set up for Carrot Con right now. This better be important!"

"Lady Beatrice is gone," Bouncer said.

Rolly looked bothered. "That's what you said on the phone."

"A rabbit took her."

Rolly laughed.

"It's true," I said. "A huge rabbit. Probably the same one that tore up those trees earlier. And now this man is waving a knife at us."

"The reason I am holding them at knifepoint is because I *know* Zeke had something to do with what happened," Bouncer announced.

"What?" Zeke said as all of us stared at him.

"You came for dinner and now she's gone. Lady Beatrice told me before you arrived that if anything odd happened, make sure they investigate you."

"Why did she say that?" Rolly asked.

"Because of their past. Plus, just months ago Zeke was a rabbit. Now a giant one takes her away. There must be a connection."

"That's a bunch of crab!" I argued. "We had nothing to do with it."

"That's true," Bouncer agreed. "You are children and therefore unable to plot or pull off such a terrifying act."

"Wait a second!" Rain protested. "I could think that up if I had a massive bunny."

"Excuse me," Bouncer said. "The adults are talking."

74

"I'm fourteen!" Rain argued.

Zeke spoke. "Listen, Rolly. You know me, and I'm telling you I had nothing to do with her being taken away. What we need to be doing is going to find her."

"You should probably read this before you do anything." Bouncer handed Rolly a folded piece of white paper.

The sheriff unfolded the paper and read it. When he was finished, he looked at Zeke and walked right up to him.

"Turn around," Rolly said.

"What?"

"Turn around."

Zeke turned around.

"What's that in your back pocket?" Rolly asked.

My uncle Zeke reached back and pulled out a thin pink wallet from his back pocket. Zeke looked as surprised to see it as the rest of us.

"I have no idea where this came from," Zeke said.

"Right." Rolly looked defeated. "Well, this letter is from my aunt. And it says that you stole her wallet and were the mastermind behind her being bothered by the bunny."

"That's a lie!" I yelled. "She's setting my uncle up."

"Remember, we've had disagreements with Zeke before," Bouncer said. "Now do as your aunt instructed and place Zeke under arrest."

Rolly looked at Zeke. He then looked at Bouncer and sighed. "Sorry, Zeke, but you need to come with me to town. Most of my officers are helping to set up Carrot Con, but I'll radio for some of them to get out here to find my aunt."

"I can't believe this." Zeke was baffled.

"You're arresting us?" I questioned angrily.

"Not you," Bouncer explained. "You're just kids."

Bouncer was the worst. He reminded me of a sponge named Phil Up from *Ocean Blasterzoids*. Phil was always talking down to young urchins and baby shrimp.

"I'm not arresting anyone," Rolly said. "I'm going to detain Zeke until I figure out what's going on. Come on, Zeke."

Rolly motioned for my uncle to get into his cop cart. I thought Zeke might try to argue or put up a fight, but he climbed on board without resisting.

"What should we do?" I yelled.

"Find the keys! Take the Squidmobile home! They can't hold me for long. In the meantime, remember Uli," he yelled back. "Issue #3!"

Zeke and Rolly sped away.

Bouncer looked down at us.

"Whatever you children do," Bouncer said, "you should do it somewhere else. There will be grown-ups coming to help Lady Beatrice. You being here is only going to complicate things."

I stared at Bouncer. "Did some kids pick on you once?

Because you really seem to have it out for us."

Bouncer reached out with his left hand and gave me the keys to the Squidmobile.

My face grew hot and red like the top of a boiled crab. "You had them?"

"I didn't want anyone taking your cart."

"Or you didn't want us to leave before the police got here," Juliet said with some fire in her words.

"Something like that." Bouncer walked off.

My friends and I hopped into the Squidmobile.

"What are we going to do?" Juliet asked.

"Something," I answered.

Rain frowned. "Sounds like a solid plan."

It wasn't, but I knew before any plan was made I needed to get to my uncle's house and take a look at Issue #3.

CHAPTER TEN

HOP COPS

When we got back to my uncle's house, Rain ran to the fridge, Juliet ran to the phone down the street to call her mom, and I ran to my uncle's bedroom and opened the large wooden trunk where he kept all of his *Ocean Blasterzoids* comics. Okay, I did check my hair also to make sure it was still just the way it should be.

The comics in the trunk were carefully organized, and I quickly found number three. I pulled it out and flopped onto my uncle's bed to flip through it.

The issue was called "To Eel and Back," and I was pretty familiar with it. In the story Admiral Uli had to visit Slither, which was a city filled with shifty eels. Someone in Slither had stolen the ocean-famous Ink Diamond.

Juliet was back from her phone call.

"Do you know why Issue #3 is important yet?" she asked.

"Not yet. I don't think there are any ink diamonds involved with Lady Beatrice getting snatched, but . . . here it is."

I showed the page to Juliet.

"Look, Eel-mo gets kidnapped, but it was actually Eel-mo that set it up."

"So, your uncle thinks Lady Beatrice and Bouncer planned it?"

"Of course," I said with excitement. "That's why the cops got there so quickly. Bouncer probably called them before it even happened."

Rain came into the room eating a banana covered with jam.

I grimaced. "That's disgusting."

"There wasn't anything else to eat." He took a big bite and chewed loudly. "Have you figured anything out?"

"I think Zeke was trying to tell us that the kidnapping was a fake."

"So what do we do?"

"Why would they want to do a fake kidnapping?" Juliet asked. "I mean, what good is it for her to be gone? And why does she want your uncle in jail? And where did the giant bunny come from?"

"Well, Zeke said she didn't like him. Maybe this whole thing is just to get back at him."

"So do we need to bust him out?" Rain asked. "The police station's pretty old. We could drive that squid car into the walls and knock them down."

"Squidmobile," I corrected.

"It doesn't matter what you call it," Juliet pointed out. "We're not breaking anyone out of jail."

"Should we go back to Lady Beatrice's house and snoop around?" I suggested. "I'm not bad at snooping."

Rain pointed to the bedroom window that looked out over the backyard and garden, and we watched in silence for a moment as the sun set over Bunny Island.

"I'm not sure that heading to that part of the island right now is a great idea."

A glowfish went off over my head.

I looked at Juliet. "Do you know how to bake?" I asked with excitement.

She put her hands on her hips and bit her lower lip. "Why, because I'm a girl?"

"No, because I don't."

"I can bake," Rain volunteered.

I should have known that. Rain's mom, Flower, ran the Liquid Love Shack, and she was really good at cooking disgustingly healthy things. I had once seen her make a plum-and-tomato pie. It made sense that some of her gross skills would rub off on Rain.

"Excellent," I exclaimed. "To the kitchen! To save Lady Beatrice and clear my uncle's good name—"

"By baking?" Juliet asked.

"Yes, my squid, by baking!" I proclaimed.

CHAPTER ELEVEN

SECRET INGREDIENT

It took way longer than I had hoped to bake what we needed. Rain knew what he was doing, but we didn't have all the ingredients. He had to run home to get what we were missing. He forgot the baking powder, so Juliet went to the neighbors' and got some.

I needed him to bake a nice cake that looked good. He did a small test cake, and after we devoured it he baked another larger one. When it was done, I added the secret ingredient, and then we frosted it with green icing. Juliet drew a white flower on top and added some pink sprinkles.

We stared at the cake as it sat on the counter.

"That looks amazing," Juliet said.

"Yeah, Rain. You should bake more often."

Rain was covered in flour and frosting and tried to not look overly proud.

It was too late to put my plan into action, so both of my friends went home, promising to be back tomorrow morning. After they were gone, I left the house and walked to the phone booth at the edge of the neighborhood. Nobody was using it, so I stepped inside and dialed my home number.

After one ring, my father picked up.

"Hello, Dad."

"Hello, Perry. I know you just left, but the house seems like an empty wheat field."

My father loved growing things and reading *The Old Farmer's Almanac*. He also loved talking about fields and seeds and wheat.

"I miss you, too, Dad."

"How's Zeke?"

"He's . . . okay."

"Nice. I tell you, growing up with him I never thought he'd turn out to be the person he is. Sure, he's a little rough around the edges, but he's good stock."

"Right, about that . . ."

"I remember when we were kids he used to smear pudding from his lunch box on my seat in the school bus. Then when I got to school, it looked like I had . . . well, like I said he's a little rough around the edges. Are you getting ready for the Rabbit Jamboree?"

"It's Carrot Con, and sort of."

"Remember, 'sort of' is sort of lame."

"Right. We had dinner with some fancy rabbit lady tonight."

My father gasped. "Lady Beatrice?"

I was surprised. "You know her?"

"There are books written about how she and her husband brought the bunnies to that island. Your uncle sent me one that I read a few years back. He used to work for her, you know. I'm surprised she let you come to dinner. According to Zeke, she doesn't care for him."

"I think that's true. She—"

"Let's not think the worst of people," he interrupted. "She did invite you over. Maybe she's had a change of heart."

"Actually, she was—"

"I think it's neat those two are getting along."

"But, you don't—"

"Exactly," he said not letting me get a word in edgewise. "You don't really know a person until you've walked a mile in their shoes."

"I hate walking."

I wanted to tell my dad about Zeke being locked up, but since he wasn't letting me I decided to wait until the morning. There was nothing he could do and no reason to worry him tonight. I figured I'd get some sleep and put my plan into action in the morning. If that failed, I could try to fill my dad in.

"*Hate* is a strong word," he said. "I'd hate for you to miss out on something just because you were afraid of a little walking."

I wasn't sure how the conversation had gotten to where it was, but I decided to steer it back to something less dumb.

"Thanks for letting me come, Dad."

My father sniffed. "You're welcome. I'm proud of you. A few months ago, you wouldn't even leave your room. Just be safe, and listen to your uncle."

"That's my plan," I said.

My father said a few more fatherly things. He also threw out a grain-related pun.

"I sure think you're pretty wheat."

When we were done talking, I hung up and returned to my uncle's house to get some sleep. I wasn't sure what tomorrow would bring, but I was sure it'd be a long day and that I needed to be like Admiral Uli in Issue #17, when he had to play tag with a herd of puffer fish—ready for anything!

OCEAN BLASTERZOIDS
SQUID OUT OF WATER

Our most powerful weapon is the element of surprise.

Nobody will be expecting us aboveground.

CHAPTER TWELVE
PASSING OFF THE CAKE

I woke up at eight the next morning and put on my Squid Squad T-shirt and some green cargo shorts. I filled my pockets with anything I thought I might need—candy bars, my limited fishdition squid goggles I had bought online a year ago, and the new mask I'd made out of another glove and rubber bands. What didn't fit, I put in a backpack along with a dozen water bottles and a flashlight that was lying on the counter in the kitchen. Stocked and ready, I headed out to pick up my friends.

Yes, friends.

I don't know why I repeated that; it's probably because I'm still getting used to having real ones. Sure, Rain was kind of a half friend, but Juliet, for sure, was a whole one. That probably explains why I picked her up first.

I arrived at her house at exactly nine o'clock. The Squidmobile was charged and ready for adventure. Juliet came out of her house looking excited and dressed for the occasion. She had on blue leggings and a white tank top over a pink shirt. Her hair was teased up, and her lips were frosted like an '80s rock star. She looked like she was ready to just have fun. She hopped on the Squidmobile.

"Are you worried?" she asked.

"I feel a bit inky," I admitted.

Juliet looked at the backseat and saw the cake sitting there.

"I'm surprised you didn't eat it last night."

"I thought about it."

I drove the Squidmobile to Rain's. It took a few minutes, but eventually he came out of his house, wearing a red tank top and white shorts. He looked bored, which made him seem even cooler.

"I can't believe I'm doing this," he told us as he got on the cart. "I have other friends, you know."

Juliet and I just stared at him. I pulled away from his house and drove past hordes of Bunny Mooners and Carrot Con visitors.

"Look at all these tourists," Rain mumbled. "I could be making major bucks taxiing people around on my bike."

"Yeah, but what we're doing will be much more exciting," I pointed out. "And we have to clear my uncle's name."

Rain looked at the cake on the seat next to him.

"I don't know," he said. "All of this seems like a bad idea."

"A lot of my ideas are questionable," I admitted. "But as Uli said once, 'Where there's a krill, there's a bay.'"

"That makes no sense," Rain said.

"It wasn't one of the better issues."

"You know, when I was younger I used to like the Marcus Money comics," Rain admitted. "That little rich kid was amazing. But then I grew up and stopped thinking about Marcus and his Money Buddies. Maybe you should give the squid thing a rest."

"Admiral Uli could destroy Marcus Money," I informed him.

Rain looked beaten. "Again, I'm not sure this is the best way to spend my day."

"Only one way to find out," I said as I pushed the gas pedal to the floor and we zipped up the stone path, swerving around a few booths and large groups of people.

"There're so many people here for Carrot Con," I shouted. "I can't believe it!"

"I know." Juliet sounded excited. "The talent show is going to be packed tomorrow. If I win, I'll probably have to travel off the island and do my talent somewhere else."

"You mean your ventriloquism?" I asked as I swerved around a patch of black rabbits.

"Yes."

Rain moaned.

"What?" Juliet said defensively. "It's a talent."

"Not really," Rain argued. "Do you have a dummy?"

Juliet looked hurt. She crossed her arms and didn't speak.

"Sorry," Rain tried. "I just don't like the dolls. Those ventriloquist dummies freak me out."

"When I was younger, I wanted to be a ventriloquist," I admitted. "My dad even made me a dummy. But I couldn't talk with my lips closed. It was just like mumbles."

Rain laughed. "What was your doll's name?"

"Knotty John."

Now Juliet was laughing, too.

"Because he was made out of knotty pine wood," I said defensively.

We pulled up to the police station and skidded to a stop at the cement block front steps. The station was actually just an old cement building that had been around for years. It was built to withstand any tropical storms. It had large open windows with no glass in them and scraggly scrub bushes all around it. On top was a flagpole with the Bunny Island flag flying on it.

I parked the Squidmobile and picked up the cake from

the backseat. We all walked into the building together, trying not to look nervous.

"I hope this works," Juliet whispered.

"If it doesn't, we're no worse off," I whispered back.

"They could lock us up for trying to aid and abet a felon," Rain said.

"Yeah, sure, there's that—but we're kids," I argued.

"Yeah, kids who are trying to sneak something in to a prisoner," Rain told me.

I know Rain was just being his usual obnoxious self, but his concern did make me a little nervous. As we entered the building, my hands were shaking while they held the cake. There was only one police person behind the counter. She was a woman with deep brown skin and bleached hair. She had on a green shirt and green shorts just like Rolly wore. Her name tag announced to the world that she was Melanie. She didn't notice us when we came in as she was trying to swat a bothersome fly. Because there was no glass in the windows, the room was breezy and buggy. A few rabbits slept in the shadows near the back door.

We stood in front of the counter, letting her finish off the fly. It took three more tries before she killed the tiny, buzzy beast.

"You don't come into my house and think you can mess with me," Melanie said aloud.

We weren't sure if she was talking to the dead fly or to us.

"What?" she asked. "What do you kids want? Is that a cake?"

"It is," I said, acting as spokesman for our group. "We made it for my uncle. He's in your jail."

"Zeke?" she asked with a smile. "Zeke's your uncle?"

We all nodded.

"Well, he's behind that door. We don't get a lot of prisoners. In fact, if he weren't here, I'd be out helping set up Carrot Con or looking for Lady Beatrice."

"So, do you know when Zeke will get out?" Juliet asked.

"I know a lot of things, but Rolly said Zeke took his aunt's wallet, so we have to keep him here until we find Beatrice and she can press charges."

"He didn't take her wallet," I insisted. "It was planted on him."

"You kids are so cute" was all Melanie had to say about that. "How about you let me have a piece of that cake before your uncle has some?"

"No, thank you," I said.

"It looks really good."

"It's for my uncle."

Melanie looked at us out of the corner of her eye. She scrunched up her face and scratched her head as if a thought was trying to work its way into her brain.

"I don't know if I should just let you give Zeke a cake. I saw a movie once where some people baked a saw into the cake so that a prisoner could saw his way through the bars and get out."

I gulped. "There's no saw in this cake."

"We promise," Juliet added.

"Well then, you won't mind if I have a piece."

Before I could stop her, she took the cake from my hands and set it down. She found a letter opener on the counter that looked like a small knife and began to push it into the cake.

My heart stopped. Juliet started to sweat.

I was about to blurt out what we had hidden in the cake when she suddenly stopped cutting.

"Wait . . ." She looked at each of us. "Does this cake have gluten in it?"

I looked at Juliet and then over at Rain.

"Why?" I managed to ask.

"Because I can't eat gluten. Swells my ankles up and makes me hard to be around."

"Well, that's what we were trying to say before. There's a lot of gluten in it," Rain spoke up.

"Tons," I said. "I added extra because I know my uncle likes it."

"Shoot, then I can't have any." She pulled the letter opener out of the icing and pushed the cake back to me.

"I guess you can give it to your uncle. He's in the cell behind that door."

Melanie nodded to a door behind the counter and waved at us to follow her. I picked up the cake and did just that. Juliet and Rain walked right behind me, not saying a word. I was sweating, but I was always sweating on Bunny Island.

Melanie opened the door and we all walked into a small space with a wall of metal bars to the right of it. Behind the bars were a couple of wooden benches hooked to the wall and two cots. Sitting on one of the benches was Zeke. He was alone and surprised to see us.

"Hey, Zeke," Melanie said in a very friendly manner. "You've got visitors."

My uncle stood up and half smiled. He looked like a caged tiger that knew he was beat. Melanie let me hand him the cake. After he took it, she shut the door and went back out front, leaving us alone with my uncle.

"We made that cake for you," I said slyly.

"Thanks, I'm starving."

"You'll have to eat it with your fist because we didn't bring you a fork."

"I love fist cake."

"Eat it carefully," I whispered while winking at the same time.

"Are you okay?" My uncle looked concerned.

"I'm fine," I replied. "I just think you should eat it . . . carefully." I winked again.

"Okay, I will." Zeke now looked confused.

"There's something extra inside," Rain said softly.

"Oh." Zeke had finally caught on. "Then I'll definitely bite down . . . carefully."

"When do you think they'll let you out?" Juliet asked.

"I don't know." Zeke sighed. "Rolly didn't act like it would be anytime soon. When we got that invitation, I thought that Beatrice was no longer mad. Now I can clearly see that she still is." Zeke looked around his small cell and growled. "I didn't take her wallet."

"Of course you didn't," Juliet said.

"She's so the worst," I said passionately. "She served us squid. And I think you're right about Issue #3. She kidnapped herself and now she's trying to ruin you."

"I think Bouncer's in on it as well," Zeke whispered. "He's done everything she said for the last thirty years. They want to cause some drama or ruin the Carrot Con. I really do have to get out of here."

"Just eat your cake," I told him. "And you might not be free, but we are."

"Until four," Rain told us. "I forgot to say, but I'm supposed to help my mom set up her booth for the Carrot Con."

"And I think you three should wait until I'm free and able to help you."

"Squids have a hard time waiting," I reminded him. "We'll just do a little snooping."

"You are good at that," my uncle admitted. "Just don't do anything your dad wouldn't approve of."

"Okay, just make sure you eat your cake."

I winked once more, and he looked even more worried.

"Is your eye okay?" he asked.

Melanie came back in and informed us that our time was up. As we were leaving the cell area and walking back around the counter, I heard the police radio crackle with life.

"Hello?" a female voice said over the radio. "Is there someone there?"

I stopped because I recognized the voice.

Melanie ran to the radio and pushed a button. "This is Melanie. Who's speaking?"

"Lady Beatrice, of course." She sounded bothered that Melanie didn't instantly recognize her voice. "I'm being held captive and using this machine to inform you that I'm okay."

Rain, Juliet, and I all stood perfectly still and listened in.

"Despite my condition," Lady Beatrice said, "the

bunnies of the island have some demands to make."

"Bunnies?" Melanie was confused.

"You are unaware, but I have the ability to talk to them at moments, and fortunately for all of us, one of those moments is now. They are going to hold me hostage until their demands are met."

Melanie got a pad of paper and a pen. "Okay, what are their demands?"

"They want every last person to leave the island. This is their home, and they demand that we give it back. If this doesn't happen, there will be war, a bunny battle royale."

Melanie was scribbling. "Their home, want it back, bunny battle royale. Got it. Wait, everyone has to leave the island?"

"Everyone." Lady Beatrice was insistent.

The radio crackled and then shut off.

Melanie looked at us.

"They didn't train me for things like this," she admitted. "I mainly just do the filing and sweep up the station. Sometimes I walk the streets cleaning up bunny poop."

"They can't evacuate the island," Juliet blurted out. "Carrot Con starts this afternoon."

Melanie grimaced. "I gotta radio Rolly."

She got back on the radio and tried to contact Rolly. The three of us slipped out of the station as fast as we could and climbed into the Squidmobile.

"You know what we've got to do?" I asked them.

"Something that doesn't keep me out past four?" Rain answered.

"Right, but we can't wait around for Zeke. We have to find Beatrice and capture that rabbit. Something's up, and we've got to figure out what before it's too late."

"Let's go, then," Juliet said excitedly.

We drove away from the police station and headed out for Furassic Park.

"By the way," I said. "Is there something wrong with my wink?"

Neither of them answered.

"You can tell me."

Rain spoke. "Let's just say that I hope your snooping is better than your winking."

I would have felt bad, but Admiral Uli wasn't a strong winker either. I took comfort in that and stomped down on the gas.

CHAPTER THIRTEEN

HEADING INTO STRANGER

Bunny Island is a great place. You should visit, but bring snacks.

Seriously, bring snacks.

I didn't think it was that wonderful at the beginning, but thanks to everything I had been through since I first arrived, I now felt different. It had grown on me like a bunch of barnacles. There was the main part of town where the wide stone paths ran alongside Rabbit Road. The road started at the airport and went all the way to the ocean. Most of the stores and restaurants and hotels were located in that section. There was also the mall where I had been turned into a rabbit not that long ago. Down by the water, there were a few neighborhoods where odd little houses like my uncle's were littered around like different-shaped blocks put out by a giant toddler with impulse control problems. There was the clearing near the Bunny Bumps and the high cliffs on the far east side where a thin rock pillar named Cottontail Tower was located. I thought I had a pretty good idea of everything that was on the island, but yesterday changed all of that. The thick jungle on the west end of the island, where Beatrice lived, felt like a whole different world. Until dinner last night, I had no reason to even know it existed. Furassic Park was big and mysterious, and I found it odd that Juliet or Rain had never filled me in on it.

"I didn't know it was there," Juliet insisted. "My parents might have mentioned it, but bunnies are so common here, I guess I didn't care."

"Yeah," Rain said as he sat in the backseat. "Lady Beatrice has a lot of pull around here, and she doesn't like people bothering her land."

"Well, we're going to bother her now."

The drive back to Beatrice's was long, and I was happy to have the Squidmobile.

"Remember when we had to run everywhere?" Juliet asked.

I shivered just thinking about it.

"You should let me drive," Rain told me. "After all, I

make a living driving people around."

"I doubt you make a living," I pointed out.

"Well, I drive people around and they pay me."

"I know. I remember when you almost killed me and then charged me too much."

"See?" Rain said. "I'm a pro."

We drove into the jungle, and the trees began to close in around us.

"Anyone else creeped out?" I asked.

Both of them nodded.

When we finally reached Beatrice's house, it was just past ten a.m., and like before there was nobody around. I thought there might be a cop car or a tent set up for the search, but there wasn't.

"Maybe everyone's out in the sanctuary looking for her," Juliet suggested.

I drove around the house, back to where the tram track was.

"Take that road!" Juliet was pointing to a small road that ran the same direction as the tracks.

It was a dirt path with trees growing on both sides that created a canopy over it. I turned and drove under the dark leaves and branches.

"So what's the plan?" Juliet asked.

"I don't really have one yet," I admitted. "I figure we

start by finding that giant rabbit and catching it."

"Seriously?! How?" Rain asked. "It was huge."

"It might be bigger than us, but it can't be smarter than us," I argued.

Rain looked at me and Juliet. "Really? I gotta think I'm the smartest one here, and a creature like that could easily outsmart me."

"We've all dealt with bunnies before."

"Yeah," Juliet agreed. "But those bunnies were normal size and cute. Remember the yellow one?"

Rain cooed and then stopped himself. "Yeah, the bunny that took Lady B was definitely not cute."

"Do you want me to tell you what Admiral Uli would do?" I asked.

"No," Rain said.

"Zeke should have found the surprise in the cake by now," Juliet said. "But if he doesn't, we have to make this right—and we don't have any time to lose if we're going to do that and still make it to Carrot Con on time."

It was dark beneath the trees, but small shards of sunshine broke through the leaves above. Everything looked like it was raining light. The Squidmobile's headlights also helped to break up the shadows.

Rain tapped me on the shoulder and spoke. "I don't

know if it's a good thing or a bad thing, but someone's following us."

I tried to look behind me, but I was driving. Juliet and Rain shifted in their seats and took a good look.

"Where?" Juliet asked.

"Way back there. Look."

"I can see the headlights," she said. "They're getting closer."

"Who is it?" I asked. "Does it look like a cop cart?"

"No, can you go any faster?" Juliet asked.

I pushed my foot all the way down, but the Squidmobile didn't go much faster.

"They're gaining on us," Rain said. He was turned around in his seat and keeping lookout.

Golf carts are actually the worst vehicles for high-speed car chases. There were no revving motors or crazy speeds. Just a low hum and the sound of the tires rolling over the dirt.

"Wait," Rain said. "I think it's . . . it's Bouncer!"

"Suction cups!" I cursed.

Bouncer was after us. His golf cart must have been better than the Squidmobile, because it was catching up.

Juliet drummed on the dash. "Go, go, go!"

"I'm go, go, going," I assured her. "The thing is, I don't even know where we're really headed! If this does lead to the bunny sanctuary, we won't be able to get in."

"Bouncer looks upset!" Rain said. "I can see his expression now, and he really doesn't look happy."

"Check under the seats!" I yelled. "Maybe there's something you can throw at him."

Rain lifted up the empty backseat next to him. Beneath it was a large storage compartment, and inside of the compartment was an umbrella and a snorkel. There was also a tennis racket and a bunch of tennis balls. Rain didn't ask permission. He just started hucking tennis balls back toward Bouncer and his Squintmobile.

The balls just bounced off his cart.

"Throw the racket!" Juliet screamed.

Rain heaved the racket, and it hit the front of Bouncer's vehicle and flew off into the trees.

"It's not helping," Rain yelled. "It's just making him angrier."

The small dirt road began to slope upward and bend. The branches above thinned out a little, and it was easier to see what was up ahead. Bouncer was close enough behind us that we could now hear him screaming.

"Stop! This instant! Stop!"

I wasn't about to listen to the man who had helped put my uncle in jail.

"Throw something else!" I ordered.

Rain shifted and lifted the seat he had been sitting on. The compartment was packed with small round bags that were filled with colorful orange dust. Rain lifted one in his hand and showed it to me.

"What are those?" I yelled.

"They're color bombs," he yelled back. "Everyone on the island has been making them for weeks. They're for the Carrot Color Battle tomorrow."

"The whole island is going to have a powder fight," Juliet added. "It looks like those are some of the ones your uncle made."

"Well, I'm not saving them for tomorrow," Rain said with a smile.

He began to rapidly throw the sacks. They hit up against Bouncer's cart and exploded into big bursts of orange. The look was fantastic, but it wasn't slowing Bouncer down. Rain hit the front of Bouncer's golf cart repeatedly and whacked Bouncer over and over with orange dust. From the way Juliet was laughing I knew it must have looked amazing.

"He looks like a squinty cheese puff!" Juliet screamed.

"Stop . . . at . . . once!" Bouncer was yelling, but he was having a difficult go at it due to the bags of powder hitting him in the face.

"They're not slowing him down enough," Rain complained.

I was nervous and sweating like a pig in polyester as the path turned again and the trees opened up even more. I saw another path heading west.

"I have an idea!" I hollered.

"Is it stupid?" Rain asked nervously.

"A little."

Bouncer was right behind us. In a few seconds, he would be crashing into the back of the Squidmobile.

"Hold on!" I shouted.

I came to the other path just as Bouncer was tapping the back of our cart with the front of his. At the last second, I turned as hard as I could onto the opposite road. I was hoping we would turn so fast that Bouncer wouldn't have time to react. He would then have to keep going on the road until he could turn around to catch back up.

That's what I was hoping for.

What happened was that I turned too quickly and the Squidmobile slid on the dirt path and tipped over. The whole thing went crashing into the trees and bushes. The impact wasn't too bad because of the thick growth on the ground. But it was a solid jolt, and the three of us ended up in a big pile, still inside the tipped-over cart.

"Are you okay?" Juliet asked as my head rang.

"I think so."

"Me, too," Rain replied. "My arm is scraped."

"That was your plan?" Juliet asked.

"Not exactly," I said lamely. "I thought—"

A voice interrupted me.

"Everybody stay where you are."

It was Bouncer. We looked up to see him standing over us. He was covered from head to toe with orange dust. Even though he was clearly upset, he still looked really festive.

"I—" I started to speak, but again my speech was cut short, this time by a large pounding thump.

All of us including Bouncer looked around. There was another thump followed by the sound of breaking branches. Then, with one big thud, a new visitor arrived.

The monster rabbit was back.

We all looked up and screamed. Like snooping, I was really good at yelling. The rabbit landed with a thud in front of Bouncer. We all gaped in amazement. But before we could even think to move, and without pausing to twitch his nose or wriggle his giant whiskers, the rabid rabbit picked Bouncer up with its tiny arm. It turned its bunny head to stare at us, and then it screamed like we were about to attack it. The big bunny, which seemed even bigger than it had been last time we saw it, pushed up and leaped out of the trees and out of our sight.

We heard him loudly hopping off. None of us said a word. We just sat there and listened to the noise growing fainter as he moved farther and farther away.

"That is one enormous rabbit," Juliet said needlessly.

"One big bun," I whispered.

We all stood up and looked at the Squidmobile as it lay on its side with two of the wheels still spinning. Part of the roof was ripped.

"Not awesome," Juliet said.

"Not at all," I agreed.

"Whatever," Rain said, frustrated. "I still need to be home by four."

The three of us tried to get the Squidmobile back on its tires. We all grunted and changed positions a dozen times, but we just weren't strong enough to tip it back up. Our ride was down, and we had nobody to blame but . . .

Okay, okay, it was all my fault.

OCEAN BLASTERZOIDS

SQUID OUT OF WATER

CHAPTER FOURTEEN
UNLOCKED AND UNNERVING

We hiked out of the trees and found Bouncer's cart. We figured since he was gone he wouldn't mind us using his wheels. Sadly, however, the keys weren't in it.

"He probably had them in his pockets when Big Bun took him," I said.

"So is that what we're calling him now?" Juliet asked.

"He is big," I pointed out. "And he's a bunny. Plus, he's got big buns. So it works on a lot of levels."

"Let's not worry about what to call him," Rain growled. "We have bigger problems—like how to get back home."

"We can't go back yet," I replied. "We have to get Zeke out, and we can't do that without Lady B."

"I don't know," Juliet spoke up. "Maybe Rain is right. Did you see how much bigger Big Bun looked?"

"It was just the angle we were at," Rain said. "We were on the ground, so of course he looked bigger."

My white Sharky-Barky chirped. The chirp was followed by the sound of my uncle's voice.

"Finally," I said with a smile.

"Perry, are you there? Under." Zeke was whispering, but we could all hear him through the Barky.

"Yes, how was the cake? Under."

"Delicious," Zeke said.

I saw Rain flash a smile about the review.

"I have to whisper so they don't hear me," Zeke hissed. "Very clever to hide this in my dessert. Are you okay? Under."

"We're fine. The Squidmobile tipped over when Big Bun jumped us and butlernapped Bouncer. Under."

I quickly filled in my uncle on everything that had happened to us since we last saw him. I also told him that we'd heard Lady Beatrice tell Melanie about all humans having to leave the island. I told him about the chase and about Rain throwing color bombs at Bouncer.

Rain took the Barky from me.

"Perry thinks we should try to find Beatrice instead of hike back," he snitched.

There was a pause.

"You have to say *under*," I whispered to Rain.

Rain grumbled. "Right, Perry thinks we should try to catch the rabbit. . . . Under."

"I think you should, too," Zeke replied. "Something weird is going on here. You need to find her so I can get released. Under."

Rain looked baffled. "No offense, Zeke, but that seems like bad advice."

Another pause.

I elbowed Rain.

"Over," he said frustrated.

"Under," I corrected.

"Under," he snapped.

"This all feels really shrimpy," Zeke said. "I can't explain it, but I'm sure Beatrice and Bouncer are up to something. I don't think they're in any danger. I think it's all part of a bigger plot that began with me being thrown in jail on trumped-up charges. You three are some of the smartest kids I know. You have to find out what's going on. Okay? Under."

Another glowfish went off over my head, and I snatched Barky back from Rain.

"I have an idea," I told my uncle. "Bouncer is covered in orange powder. So we'll just follow the trail of dust. Under."

"Good. Be careful and keep your Barky on. I gotta go. Under."

My Barky went silent.

I looked at Rain. He sighed and then spoke.

"My mom will be mad, but I guess this is more exciting than serving smoothies to Bunny Mooners. Under."

"You don't have to say *under* anymore," Juliet told him.

"Right, then let's get this over."

The three of us found the faint trail of orange-colored dust that marked the way Big Bun and Bouncer had gone. There were also plenty of broken branches and large paw prints to guide the way.

"So, Bouncer's bad?" Juliet asked as we tracked our prey.

"Yes," I said with authority.

"And that bunny woman's good?" Rain asked.

"No, she's horrible, too. But we have to find her so she can clear Zeke and get him out of jail."

The trail of powder led back to the path. After we'd walked it for five minutes, the path became very steep. My legs burned, and right before I began complaining for the sixth time, the path leveled out, giving me some relief. I could now see part of the tall sanctuary walls and pointed it out to my friends.

"We have eyes, too," Rain reminded me.

I think that was Rain's way of saying *thank you*.

The three of us kept following the clues on the road, and the trail of orange and trampled branches led us to the sanctuary walls. The color ended right in front of a wall that was taller and more intricate than anything I'd ever seen before. It ended at a large metal gate shaped like a rabbit with ears sticking straight up. There was a huge latch on the gate that looked like a small rabbit head with no ears. Hanging on the gate were three small metal rods.

Rain scratched his head. "I don't think even Big Bun could have hopped over that."

"In one issue of *Ocean Blasterzoids*, Admiral Uli has to climb over the wall that surrounds Tuna Town. Of course, he has suction cups and tentacles."

Juliet walked to the gate, grabbed the bunny-head knob, and pulled.

It was locked.

I stepped up and took a closer look.

"Weird," I said quietly. "What are the holes on the top of its head?"

"Maybe there were some little ears and they broke off," Rain suggested.

I stuck two of my fingers in the holes.

"Or maybe it's like the time Admiral Uli looked into the pool holes near Manta Bay"—I was excited—"and he saw the way to dismantle that newtlear bomb?"

I leaned down and looked into the holes on top of the knob. There was nothing but an inky darkness.

Luckily, Juliet was more levelheaded than me. She

grabbed ahold of two of the small metal rods hanging on the gate and stuck one in each hole. The small head now looked like a complete bunny.

She tried to twist the knob, and it didn't move.

"They're not even," I pointed out. "One rod's longer."

Juliet grabbed two small rods that were the same size. She put them into the holes. This time as she turned the knob, it clicked open.

"Nice," I whispered.

"Come on," Rain said. "We haven't got time to waste."

"Wait." I was surprised to hear myself speaking. I wanted to go in, but standing near the tall wall made me suddenly feel more chicken than squid. "This is a good idea, right?"

"Not at all," Rain said. "But your uncle needs our help, so let's stop messing about and get to work, okay?"

Juliet turned the knob farther and pulled open the large metal rabbit gate. We stepped into a small space with another metal gate that was identical to the first. After closing the one we had walked through, we opened the second one. Once we were inside, I shut the second gate.

We were in.

But where were we?

The sanctuary looked positively mountainous from our vantage point. It was filled with oddly shaped hills with plastic tubes running between them. Directly in front of us was a clearing, a field, with a large old moving truck rusted in the middle. Beyond it were a few small and run-down buildings. I could make out what appeared to be a gift shop, long-ago abandoned, with broken windows and vines growing over it. Across the road from it, nearer to the gate, were a garage and toolshed. The garage door hung open, and inside stood a couple of old trucks, and the shed was practically hidden behind wooden barrels topped with rusted tools.

There was no sign of any bunnies anywhere, which made the scene feel extra creepy.

Juliet shouted, "Over there!"

I could see where the faint trail of orange dust picked back up. All three of us looked back at the wall and did the same calculation.

"Wow," Rain said for all of us. "That was a huge jump."

We followed the trail past the abandoned gift shop and between two large, rabbit-shaped hills, toward the plastic tunnels that looked like a playground tube slide. They were easily big enough for a person to climb through. The whole place was like a total bunny fantasy land—but with no sign of bunnies.

Juliet poked me and pointed to two rusty metal "hamster wheels." I walked over to one of them and tried to make it move by running. It squeaked but wouldn't spin fast enough to be any fun.

"So people would come here and act like bunnies?" Rain asked.

"I guess some did . . . before it closed."

"I wish this place were still working," Juliet said.

The orange dust wound through hills and led up to the front of a large tunnel that went directly into a fat hill. There were tunnels and holes all over the place, but this one was taller than I was, wider than a car, and darker than I like my tunnels to be.

I gulped.

"I don't think we should go in there." Juliet was serious.

"Me neither," Rain chimed in.

"We're not going to," I whispered.

I was just as nervous as both of them, but fortunately for all of us I had a plan.

"Wait, do you have a plan?" Rain asked. I nodded. "Is it based on one of your comic books?"

"Of course, it is," I said. "*Ocean Blasterzoids* #35: 'To Catch a Carp.' We're going to build a trap."

CHAPTER FIFTEEN
HARE SNARE

Not far from the field with the rusted truck was a pile of junk and leftover building supplies. There were also a number of separate plastic tube segments—long, round pieces that could be connected to make a slide or a tunnel.

Of course, I had other plans for them.

"Keep your eyes open," I warned Rain as we both carried sections of the tubing over to the rusted truck. "I don't want to be ambushed by any massive bunnies or angry newts."

"I don't see any bunnies, and I haven't seen a single newt," he replied.

"That doesn't mean they're not there. Newts, salamanders, squids, they're all good at camouflaging themselves. There could be a ning of newts hiding right on that hill."

Rain looked skeptical. "A ning?"

"There's no special name for a group of newts, so I call them a ning. It sounds like something they would be called."

"It sounds stupid," Rain said.

"Exactly," I agreed.

"I think it's a good name," Zeke said from the Barky I had hooked to my belt. "Under."

My uncle had been talking to us whenever he could. He had told us that Sheriff Rolly had gotten another message from Beatrice insisting that all people needed to be off the island by tomorrow.

"So, is the sheriff going to evacuate the island?" I asked. "Under."

"No," Zeke replied. "But he seems worried. I think inky times are ahead. Under."

It was good to hear Zeke's voice, but we all wished that he were here to help us move things. It was hot, humid, and I was getting way more physical activity than I had ever wanted.

"Someone's coming," Zeke said suddenly from back at the police station. "I have to go. Under."

The Barky went silent.

When we got to the truck, Juliet was there tying knots

in some rope we had found. The tools we had taken from the shed were lying on the ground and ready to be used. The three of us had also broken off one of the big running wheels and managed to roll it over to work on.

"It's time to build," I said.

Juliet had a Sharpie in her backpack, and we drew out our blueprint for the trap on the side of the old truck. The idea was loosely based on the board game Rat Grab. We would lure Big Bun out of the tunnel, and when he came out he would step on the rakes we'd spread around. The rake handles would flip up and hit him on the head as they yanked up the rope that would be attached to a rock that would fling it into the air so that it would land on a seesaw we'd made from a long board and barrel. On the other end of the seesaw, we placed a round piece of plastic tunnel, which would be launched into the air by the rock and slide onto Big Bun's head. Disoriented, Big Bun would then stumble over an assortment of old yard tools, perfectly positioned to make it hard for him to hop away. Then two long boards would swing in from the sides, forcing him into the back of the truck, where we'd lock him up. The plan seemed solid to me, but when we finally finished setting things up it didn't look quite the same as the drawing. Honestly, it looked more like a junk yard with bits connected by rope and tools.

"I don't know," Rain said. "If this works, I'll never say

any of your plans are stupid again. That's how confident I am that this will never work."

"I'm gonna say I'm having my doubts as well," Juliet admitted.

"It's going to work," I promised them.

"So how are we going to get Big Bun here?" Rain asked.

I motioned for them to follow me.

We walked to the shed where the tools had been. Inside the shed in the corner were two huge wooden barrels. They were sealed up and both of them had the word *pellets* painted on the side of them.

"Help me get these out."

Rain tipped one of the barrels over and rolled it out. Juliet and I rolled the other one. They were heavy and full of rabbit food. We put the barrels at the beginning of our trap where the rakes were. Then, using a rusty hammer and crowbar, we made a hole in the top of one of them. We tipped the barrel over on its side and spilled out the grassy-green pellets near the opening.

"Perfect," I exclaimed.

Rain rolled the barrel away from the trap and toward the hills, leaving a line of pellets in his wake. Juliet and I followed to the side of him with our still-closed barrel. When the pellets in Rain's barrel ran out, we cracked open ours and continued the line all the way up to the foot of the large tunnel that Big Bun had gone into.

"He'll smell these pellets," I explained. "Then he'll come out of his tunnel and follow them all the way into the trap."

"I don't know," Rain said. "What if he's not hungry?"

"Also," Juliet said, sounding worried. "He'd better hurry before they're all gone." She was looking back toward the direction of the trap. All along the trail of pellets, there were now regular-size rabbits eating the bait.

"No," I hollered while waving my arms. "It's not for you."

Rain ran to scare some off, but they barely moved.

I was flipping out trying to scare off the normal-size bunnies, but then the sound of something rising from behind us in the huge tunnel caused us all to turn our heads and look back into the large black hole.

Frummp!

Frummp!

"We should probably run," I whispered.

"We should *definitely* run," Juliet whispered back.

We took off just as Big Bun's big head popped out. His nose was twitching, and his eyes glowed red. He began hopping toward the pellets.

"Get to the trap!" I yelled.

It was harder to run back to the trap than I'd thought it would be. There were thousands of rabbits now trying to snarf down the pellets we had spilled out. I kept stumbling over bunnies as I ran. It also didn't help to hear Big Bun loudly screeching as he hopped along the pellet trail.

When we got to the trap, all of us took our places. Juliet and Rain were manning the long wooden boards to corral Big Bun into the truck. And I was in charge of closing the truck doors once he was in. As soon as I was in my spot, I looked back and saw Big Bun coming out from behind the hills and pushing away smaller rabbits as he sucked up pellets like a hop-vac.

"Are you ready?!" I yelled.

Both Juliet and Rain yelled back yes.

The bunny monster was hopping closer. As he moved into position, I saw that he was forcing hundreds of regular-size rabbits toward the trap with him. They were all scrambling to get out of his way. My heart skipped a beat, knowing that if the smaller rabbits got to the trap first, they might set things off and ruin the whole thing.

Big Bun took another huge hop and chomped down on more pellets. Then with a scream he hopped again. As he landed, his right foot hit one of the rakes and sent the handle flying up into the air. The handle pulled the rope, which released the rock, which landed perfectly on the seesaw. Big Bun jumped sideways and hundreds of smaller rabbits crowded around him. They set off the other rakes, which messed with the position of the seesaw.

The board was now crooked and flung the plastic section of tube up into the air and toward Rain. He was standing in his position and the section of tube dropped down on him. It slid over his head and down around his torso, binding his hands to his sides, leaving only his head and legs free. He couldn't help but release the board he was in charge of early. It swung wildly and hit Big Bun in its big butt. The scream Big Bun emitted was deafening. Juliet released her board to cover her ears and it smacked at least a hundred rabbits, who went flying into the air. The rabbits rained down on us as Big Bun continued to screech. Rain tipped over in his tube and couldn't move. I ran to him and rolled him toward the back of the truck, where the doors were open.

"Get me out of this!" he screamed.

Big Bun's ears twitched, and he turned his head to look at me and Rain. I know rabbits aren't supposed to be particularly smart, but it looked like Big Bun knew that we were the cause of the trouble and now he wanted to make us pay.

Juliet ran up and helped me roll Rain. We rolled him like a barrel with his head sticking out of one side of the tube and his feet sticking out of the other. We heaved him into the empty back of the large truck. Big Bun shook and sent more rabbits into the air and moved in our direction.

"Get in!" I screamed.

"I already am," Juliet screamed back.

I looked and saw that she was in the back of the truck with Rain. I scurried up after her and pulled one of the back doors closed.

Big Bun leaped closer.

"Close the other!" Juliet yelled.

I grabbed the second door, and as I was pulling it closed, Big Bun leaped forward with his mouth open and eyes on fire. His head slammed into the door, shutting it for me. His jump had been so forceful that his two teeth had pierced the back of the metal door and were now sticking inside. His impact had also jammed the doors shut. He pulled his teeth back out and screamed. It was dark inside the truck, but a small shaft of daylight shot in from the hole his teeth had caused.

I held my breath, too scared to move and unsure if we were safe. We could hear the monster rabbit moving around outside of the truck. His eye appeared through the hole, and both Juliet and I screamed.

Big Bun banged up against the doors, but they were wedged shut due to the force of his impact. He hopped around the truck and scratched and bit at the sides. His teeth made a few more holes in the sides, but he couldn't get to us. It seemed like forever, but eventually he stopped trying and hopped off and we were able to exhale.

"Would you get me out of this?" Rain growled.

The round section of tube he was stuck in was too tight for him to squeeze out of. With a lot of effort and some swearing on Rain's part, we were able to get him up onto his feet, but we still couldn't get the tube off him.

"Perfect," he said as he stood there with his arms bound and looking like he was trapped in a straw. "I told you your plan was dumb."

"You might have been right this time," I admitted, realizing that if our goal had been to capture the rabbit, we'd only wound up catching ourselves.

Juliet and I tried to get the doors to open, but they were jammed shut. We were officially trapped.

"Did Big Bun look even larger than when he carried Bouncer off?" I asked them.

Juliet nodded slowly as she realized he had. Rain just shook his head and swore.

CHAPTER SIXTEEN
TRAPPED LIKE SARDINES

Juliet moved away from the metal doors and let me take another look at the large holes Big Bun's teeth had made. I could see all the pieces of the trap we had set lying all over the ground. Normal-size rabbits were hopping around and looking for any last pellets that may have been left behind. I sighed like a sad squid and turned back to my friends. According to my watch it was now five in the afternoon. Luckily, Juliet and I had been wearing our backpacks when we were trapped. So at least we had some water bottles. I also had a couple of candy bars in my pants pockets that I reluctantly shared.

The holes in the sides of the truck let air come through and helped prevent the confined space from heating up too much. I still would have preferred to be outside and sweating, but at least we were alive.

"I've got to get this off," Rain said for the thousandth time.

He was starting to get really stiff from being unable to bend his waist or move his arms. We had tried to free him a hundred times, but it was hopeless with what we had on us.

"We need to call your uncle Zeke," he insisted.

"If we do, the cops might hear it," I reminded him. "We have to wait until he contacts us so we know he's alone."

"This is horrible," Rain complained. "Imagine having no use of your arms."

"I'm already upset that I don't have ten tentacles like Uli."

Juliet was looking out of one of the other holes. "All the rabbits seem to be making their way back into their tunnels."

She moved to the back doors and tried again to push at them. They still didn't budge.

"This is so bad," she said. "I'm supposed to be in the talent show tomorrow."

"I'm supposed to be helping my mom serve smoothies at her booth."

"Well, I'm supposed to not be locked in an old truck,"

I pointed out. "We have to figure things out. Let's think about what we know."

"How did I ever end up in a mess like this?" Rain was upset and needed to talk. "Beatrice and Bouncer are nuts. They somehow created a giant rabbit, and now we're all doomed. Why? Why?!? WHY?!?!?"

"Maybe the two of them are in love," Juliet said, "and they just want some privacy."

Rain and I made faces.

"In love with rabbits, maybe," I told her. "I bet that tunnel they're in isn't really just a tunnel. It's probably the way to their evil headquarters. Bouncer wanted that rabbit to take him. He wanted us to be scared and turn back to town."

Juliet spoke. "Maybe you *should* try your uncle, because we need help. Even if they catch him using his walkie-talkie, at least the police will know we're trapped and send some help."

"It's a Sharky-Barky," I corrected her.

I knew Juliet was right. There was no way out of the moving truck, and nobody knew where we were. It wouldn't be the worst thing for them to discover my uncle had a Barky and that we slipped it to him in a cake. Then they could come and arrest us and at least we'd be in a jail cell instead of a dark, warm truck with not a lot of water or food.

"Fine." I gave in. "I'll try to radio him."

"So you'll listen to Juliet but not me?" Rain complained.

"Yes."

I took the Barky off my belt and pushed the button once. There was a small beep, and I spoke.

"Are you there? Under."

There was only silence.

"Try again," Juliet said.

I pressed the button and waited for the beep. "Uncle Zeke? Under."

Rain was irritated. "Seriously, can't you just say *over* like normal people?"

"You know my uncle and I aren't normal."

The Barky beeped, and we all jumped.

"Perry," I heard my uncle whisper. "They're going to hear this. Are you okay? Under."

"We're not okay," I told him. "We're trapped in the back part of Furassic Park. In a big moving truck. We were attacked by Big Bun. Under."

"I don't know . . ."

My uncle stopped speaking, and we could hear some other voices in the background at the jail. The Barky went quiet.

"What happened?" Rain asked. "He didn't say *under*."

I tried a few more times to contact him, but nobody

answered. Rain stomped his feet and danced around angrily. His small tantrum caused him to slip and fall onto his side. He then rolled around inside the truck. Seeing him like that gave me an idea.

"Juliet, get on the other side."

I stepped around Rain and got behind him.

"What?" she asked.

"Come here." I started to roll Rain toward the jammed door.

"What are you doing?" he yelled.

"We're going to slam you into the doors," I told him. "Maybe this tube is strong enough to pop them open."

Juliet had joined me, and we began to roll Rain in earnest.

"You . . . can't . . . ram . . . meeee!" Rain hollered as we pushed him along the slightly sloping floor. "Stop it!"

He was gaining speed, and we pushed even harder. The plastic tube was thick and strong, and it didn't seem like the worst idea until he slammed into the doors and it shook the entire truck.

It was quiet again, but the doors were still closed.

Rain started to really scream. He was mad—and more than a little dizzy—but he wasn't hurt. I was about to apologize to him when I noticed that there was now a small crack of light between the two doors.

"Hey," I yelled happily. "I think it's working."

Juliet saw the light.

"Let's do it one more time!" I said.

"Nooooo!" Rain screamed.

He kicked with his legs to get us to stop, but it was no use. We rolled him back as fast as we could at the front of the truck, then we climbed over him and did it again and again. Rain was yelling and throwing out threats, but I figured we would ask for forgiveness later.

"Push, Juliet!" I yelled.

"No!" Rain yelled back.

And finally, on the fourth or fifth try, the doors popped open with a terrific crack. Rain rolled right out of the truck and onto the grassy field. Juliet and I burst out behind him clapping and cheering.

Rain came to a stop against the very seesaw that had flung the tube on him earlier.

"Stand me up!" he yelled.

(He yelled a few more things, too, but they mainly had to do with me, and they weren't particularly flattering.)

Juliet and I got him onto his feet.

"Are you okay?" she asked.

"No, I'm not okay. I'm trapped in a tube!" he said, which was true. But at least he wasn't trapped in a tube trapped in a truck anymore.

It was a very small comfort.

OCEAN BLASTERZOIDS
SQUID OUT OF WATER

CHAPTER SEVENTEEN
TUNNELS ARE NO FUNNEL

After Rain finished yelling at us, we stood there wondering what to do next. Luckily, or unluckily, we didn't have to wonder long.

"Did you feel that?" Juliet asked.

"You mean the ground shaking?" I asked back.

The ground shook again, and I yelped accordingly. Far off in the distance, we could see Big Bun jumping over some hills and heading away from where we were.

"Where's he going?" Juliet asked.

"To town," I said. "Do you know what this means?"

"What?" Rain said impatiently. "Something to do with a squid?"

"No," I replied. "I mean, I wish. It means that Big

145

Bun is not in the tunnels. Which means now is the perfect time to search them."

Juliet and Rain followed me as I ran down the same trail that we'd laid with pellets. When I reached the front of the large tunnel, we stopped and caught our breath.

"We can't go in there." Rain was out of breath and patience for me. "Are you crazy?"

"Squids don't go crazy. Besides, you'll be safer than the two of us. That tube is like armor. Nobody can hurt you while you're wearing it."

"They can tip me over!"

"Then stay out here and be our guard," I offered. "If Big Bun returns, whistle. Try to imitate the sound of air moving through a squid's funnel."

I demonstrated the noise, but neither of my friends seemed impressed.

Juliet looked confused. "That won't help anything."

"Listen, I'm scared, too," I admitted. "But we'll go in quick and see what we can find. If there's nothing, we'll hightail it out of there and begin walking home. But Beatrice radioed the police station from somewhere. I believe this tunnel is their headquarters."

I took the flashlight out of my backpack and flipped it on.

I used to be scared of things like newts and outdoors, but now I had a hard time not walking up to trouble and poking it. One of the worst things about going back home to Ohio after I had been here was that there was no trouble or mystery. I had thought my neighbor was running an illegal clam ring, but after a couple of weeks of snooping and sleuthing it had turned out that he just smelled like old fish. Even still, I was proud of myself for facing up to my fears. I was turning into a proper squid, and like Admiral Uli, I was out for ink. Now, as we stood before a dark tunnel, I was fearful, but I was determined to figure things out.

"Come on." I stepped into the tunnel and motioned for them to follow.

The tunnel was so big it almost felt like a cave. The walls and ceiling were dirt with roots sticking out of them and pieces of bark and pebbles on the ground. Juliet was beside me and Rain, who had decided to come along. The three of us moved slowly, with me shining the light to lead the way.

"My life was much more boring before you arrived," Juliet whispered.

"I almost never left my room before you guys," I whispered back.

"I had use of my arms before hanging out with the two of you," Rain complained.

"Is that a light up there?" Juliet asked.

Up ahead, there was a small glow coming from around

a turn in the tunnel. We moved slowly, and when we got around the bend we could see that it was a large, rectangular room with wooden walls and plush rugs on the floor. Near one of the walls there was a long table with a glowing lamp on it. I shut off the flashlight and the room was still well lit. Next to the lamp was a radio and a few other electronic-looking things. There were two more tables covered with test tubes and glass bowls. In the corner nearest to us, there were two big, comfortable-looking chairs.

"Soft, itchy underbelly!" I exclaimed quietly but with excitement. "I was right about the secret headquarters."

"I can't believe it," Rain said. "You were."

"Where is Beatrice?" Juliet asked. "And Bouncer?"

Looking around the room, we could see three tunnels heading off into other directions.

"I'm not sure, but I bet we could use that radio to call the police for help," I whispered. "If we tell Melanie that this is all just some weird hoax, maybe she'll let Zeke go."

"Fine," Juliet said. "Do it quick. Then let's get out of here. This place is the opposite of awesome."

To make things even less awesome, we could now hear the sound of someone coming from one of the other tunnels.

Juliet and I tipped Rain over and hid him behind the big chairs as quickly as we could. We ducked down next to him to hide ourselves. I could hear two voices growing nearer. One of them was Beatrice. I thought the other would be Bouncer, but it didn't sound like him. I peeked between the chairs and saw them coming out of the tunnel and into the room. The man with Beatrice was short and bald. I'd never seen him before. He had on a white lab coat and round glasses. Beatrice looked like a mess. Her hair was sticking up wildly, and her dress was rumpled and tinged with dirt.

She walked directly to the radio.

"Don't use that," the bald man said. "You're upset. Wait till you've cooled down and you can communicate calmly."

Beatrice farted—I mean bubbled.

"What did you say, Neil? How dare you tell me to calm down," she snipped. "I'm just fine. If you had better control of that rabbit, we wouldn't be in this mess."

"I'm sorry. It's growing at an alarming rate, and the collar isn't working."

"It was supposed to scare the town into leaving the island. Now who knows what it'll do."

"I'm sure it's still scaring the town at the moment," Neil said. "It's just we have no control of it."

"I hired you to solve my problems." Beatrice harrumphed and bubbled simultaneously. "The purple carrots we used to turn people into rabbits were a bust and blew up in our faces. Now this. It might serve our purpose, but if we can't control him and he keeps on growing, the whole island could be destroyed!"

"We're not done for," Neil insisted. "We have other tricks."

Beatrice flipped on the radio and pushed a few buttons. She picked up the microphone and spoke into it.

"Hello. Hello. This is Lady Beatrice. Is anyone there?"

After a couple of moments of silence, I recognized Melanie's voice saying, "I'm here still."

"Where is the sheriff? Where's Rolly?"

"He's on Rabbit Road, helping at the Carrot Con."

Beatrice fumed. "Has he begun the evacuation?"

"Um . . . I don't think so," Melanie answered. "Last I heard, he was eating carrot dogs and helping with crowd control. That big rabbit just hopped through the town again. It's a really great promotional tool. What's it made out of?"

"I didn't make it," Beatrice screamed. "It's real."

"It is real neat," Melanie said.

"This isn't a joke," Beatrice insisted.

"I told Rolly you said that," Melanie replied.

A small metal controller in Neil's hand began to beep.

"He's coming back," Neil said nervously.

Beatrice flipped off the radio without saying

good-bye and spun around to face Neil. "This is an epic failure!"

"By my calculations," Neil said, "if it returns here, it'll probably rest for a short while and then take off back into town. It might not have hurt anyone yet, but I can't promise it won't start."

"I didn't want to hurt anyone," Beatrice said. "It's just supposed to scare everyone off the island, so that I can have a little peace and quiet and my rabbits can have their home back."

She bubbled like she was scared.

I started to laugh and put my hand over my mouth to stifle the noise.

"What was that?" Beatrice snapped. "I heard something. Over there, behind the chairs."

Neil ran across the room and reached down behind the chairs. He grabbed me by the collar of my shirt and pulled me up.

"Let go!" I yelled. "Run, Juliet!"

I threw her the flashlight, and she caught it as she was jumping up. Neil reached for her with his free hand, and she kicked him in the shins. He screamed and she darted out of the room and back down the tunnel we had come through.

"Forget about her," Lady Beatrice said. "Bring that boy over here. And what's that lying on the ground?"

Neil pulled up Rain and then dragged both of us over to Lady Beatrice.

"Children," she cursed. "What a nuisance." Beatrice stared at Rain. "What are you doing in one of my bunny's tube sections? Tomfoolery. You boys shouldn't be here."

"We came to see what happened to you," I said. "Now it's clear that you really are the one causing all the trouble."

"Me?" Beatrice held her hand to her heart. "My dear boy, it is you and every other person on this island who are causing the trouble. This island belongs to the bunnies, and you are all ruining that."

Beatrice shivered, bubbled, and then burped.

"It is my responsibility to make sure that the bunnies get their island back. We built Furassic Park to protect as many as we could. We thought people would appreciate our efforts. But it cost a lot of money to staff a place like this. And when the donations dried up, we had to close it from the public and start thinking up new ways to protect the rabbits from you humans. You just want to build and play and run around—without thinking about how it affects the bunnies who live here. We used to have dozens of scientists working on ways to keep the bunnies safe and happy and healthy. Now we just have Neil."

"Thanks a lot," Neil said.

I could see Bouncer coming out of one of the tunnels

behind them. I thought about punching Neil in the stomach and making a run for it, but I wasn't sure Rain could keep up, and with Bouncer here I knew we wouldn't both get away.

"Let them go," Bouncer said.

Beatrice and Neil turned their heads around and dropped their jaws.

"How did you get out of that cage?" Beatrice snapped. "I thought we locked you up."

"I dug through the dirt walls," he said. "Now let these boys go."

"You are my butler," Beatrice said. "I don't take commands from you."

"I *used to be* your butler," Bouncer said.

"That's right." Beatrice smiled and her pale face looked like a MoonPie. "I fired you right before I locked you up."

Bouncer looked at me and Rain. "I didn't know what she was doing," he said. "I thought I was helping, but when I found out she was planning to use the monster to terrorize the island I decided to stop her. I was chasing you kids on the road because I wanted to tell you what I had discovered. But before I could tell you, I was picked up by that beast!"

"He's not a beast," Beatrice snapped. "He is a marvel. And it's too late for any of you to do anything. The rabbit is on the loose, and I suppose it's only a matter of time before he tears up the town and has everyone fighting to get off the island. Soon this place will become the bunny heaven my late husband, Owence, and I dreamed about."

Neil's remote beeped again.

"The bunny's getting closer," Neil said. "And it's not obeying anything I tell it anymore."

Neil and Bouncer looked nervous. Beatrice just looked awful. She bubbled and laughed. For a woman with such high standards, she sure seemed like she was having a total breakdown.

"It's not funny," Neil informed her. "By my calculations, the rabbit is making up its own mind now. The collar must be completely malfunctioning."

"Fine," Beatrice replied. "Then it's out of our hands and the island will get what it deserves."

"Actually," Neil said, "we should probably get out of this tunnel before it gets back. Who knows what he will do if he finds us here."

Rain and I decided to start running. We didn't wait for permission. Neil wasn't holding on to me any longer, and we knew our way out. If Big Bun was coming, I didn't want to be anywhere near him. Also, Juliet was out there, and even if she didn't need my help, I might need hers.

I ran down the tunnel toward the exit. Rain had gotten pretty good at keeping up with the tube on. Under any other circumstances, I would have thought it was hilarious to watch him run like that, but not only was it dark, his condition was sort of my fault. So I kept my laughing to myself.

We could see the exit of the tunnel where the light was coming in. I sighed with relief when I saw Juliet standing at the entrance waiting for us.

"Are they chasing you?" she yelled.

"No, and Bouncer's not . . ."

Before I could finish my sentence, we saw a giant brown paw slam down next to Juliet outside of the tunnel. The ground shook, and a large furry arm picked her up.

CHAPTER EIGHTEEN
A HAREY SITUATION

Juliet kicked and screamed as she was hoisted up by Big Bun.

When we got to the opening of the tunnel and looked up, my stomach began to spoil. Big Bun was more like Massive Bun. He was huge, just enormous, bigger than he was even just a few hours ago, and holding Juliet in his right paw. He looked down at me and Rain and screeched. Bunny saliva flew everywhere as his red eyes blinked and he whipped his whiskers through the air. The control collar around his neck had become too small and was choking him. With a snap, it finally busted apart and fell off. I was so scared that if Rain's arms hadn't been trapped in the plastic tube, I would have tried to hold his hand. Big Bun's big teeth chattered, and then with one massive stomp he stood up to his full height and hopped away toward town, holding Juliet.

Bouncer and Neil came rushing out of the tunnel then and stood next to us as we watched Big Bun bound away.

"It's got Juliet!" I told them. "And it's heading to town."

Neil was fidgeting with the remote control in his hand.

"That's not going to help," I yelled. "The collar busted and flew off."

"By my calculations, that's a problem."

Rain looked at Neil with disgust. "And people think kids are the problem."

"We've got to get to town!" I said frantically. "He has Juliet."

"Follow me," Bouncer said.

"I'm coming, too." It was Lady Beatrice, and she was standing behind Bouncer.

"Fine," Bouncer said. "But you're not my boss. And you're not in charge. Understand?"

Lady Beatrice looked impressed with Bouncer being so bold.

"I understand," she said. "I just want to make sure no bunnies are harmed."

I thought we were all going to have to run to Bouncer's golf cart, but instead we ran to the old garage and he unlocked the garage door. Bouncer threw the door open, and there was an old tractor and a large truck with a big water tank on the back.

"Does the truck work?" Rain asked.

"It runs," Bouncer said. "And it's faster than any golf cart. Get in."

We all climbed into the truck. It had two rows of seats, but it was still crowded because we had to put Rain in at an angle. He was in the backseat, leaning on Neil, and I was in the front between Beatrice and Bouncer, who was driving.

He turned the key, and the vehicle wheezed and puffed and then finally started up. He pulled out of the garage and drove across the fields where we had set up our trap and toward the front of the sanctuary. The big water tank on the back of the truck was full, and we could hear the water sloshing as the truck drove.

"What's the water in the tank for?" I asked, wondering if perhaps Beatrice was really a newt and she needed a truck that transported freshwater.

"It's actually fertilizer," Bouncer yelled. "They spray it around the sanctuary to feed some of the plants. There used to be a full-time sprayer on the staff, but now there's only a few people who look after this place."

Lady Beatrice was bothered. "Stop it. It's impolite to talk about personal matters. Especially with children."

"They're not personal matters anymore," Bouncer

said. "I'm a free man, and I can talk about whatever I want. For example, I don't like the décor in your house."

Beatrice looked wounded.

We came to the large wall, and Neil and I got out and opened a huge wooden gate so the truck could get out. We closed it after Bouncer drove through and then hopped back into the truck.

The path we were on was so narrow and the trees around it were so close that the truck scraped the branches on both sides as we drove to town.

"I hope Juliet's okay," I yelled.

"Well," Beatrice said in a snippy way, "I hope everyone's scared to death and leaving the island."

"You're a horrible person," I told her.

"You're a child, so it doesn't matter."

Lady Beatrice reminded me of Ana Porpoise. She was Admiral Uli's classmate in school. She thought she was better than everyone else and that her main purpose as a porpoise was to make decisions for everyone else. Uli didn't like her, and neither did I. Now I was sitting by the human version of a porpoise person, and I was hoping that her door might pop open and she would fly out. Juliet needed us. That was all that mattered, I kept telling myself, even if all I could think about was how much I wanted to get away from Beatrice.

"Are you going as fast as you can?" I asked Bouncer.

He nodded.

We were going way faster than any golf cart. And the Fertilizermobile was breaking branches off trees and bouncing wildly on the road. I turned around and saw that all the jostling had caused Rain to spin in his seat and he was now being forced to stare out the back window at the fertilizer tank.

"Should we go to the police station?" I asked. "Maybe we can get them to use the island sirens to warn people. We could also get Zeke out."

"No," Beatrice insisted. "He's a troublemaker, and I want him locked away."

Bouncer turned onto a new path, and the trees began to thin out, making it easier to drive.

"Why do you hate my uncle?"

"He used to work for me," she yelled. "There was an incident! He was helping me organize my books and accounting. I borrowed a few thousand dollars from some of the donations for some personal things and he got mad at me."

I turned my head and stared at her.

"What do you know?" she snapped. "It was money that someone had donated to the sanctuary, so it was every bit mine. I had to let him go after that, of course."

"So he was being honest?"

"And impertinent."

"I don't know what that means."

"It's the proper way to say he was being a total snot."

The truck bounced through the trees getting closer to town. I kept my eyes open for any sign of flying people or trees that Big Bun was throwing around. I leaned over Beatrice and rolled down the passenger-door window.

"I wanna listen out for screaming," I yelled.

Buildings began to appear, and I could see hotels and the outline of the airport. Bouncer slowed down and drove across the stone path that ran along Rabbit Road. There were booths and people everywhere. Carrot Con had officially begun.

"Where do I go?" Bouncer asked.

"I see you're not good at making your own decisions yet," Beatrice bullied him.

"No talking," Bouncer snapped.

As we got closer, we could hear screaming. People were running down the street looking for shelter, seeming terrified and confused. In the distance, I could see Big Bun leap through the air and land on Rabbit Road not far from the world-famous bunny-shaped hotel.

Bouncer slammed on the brakes.

"It's still getting bigger!" Neil wailed.

Beatrice clapped.

"Spin me around!" Rain demanded. "I want to see!"

I leaned over into the backseat and helped Neil twist

Rain's plastic tube around. Big Bun stood on his hind legs and chirped so loudly that one of the truck windows shattered. He was still holding Juliet tightly in his front paw. She was pounding her fists, kicking her feet, trying desperately to get free. She might have been screaming— I can't imagine that she wasn't—but I couldn't tell from all the noise.

"You created it," I yelled at Neil and Beatrice. "You have to know how we can stop it!"

"The problem is that we used extracted compounds from rabbits' teeth to create a growth serum," Neil answered proudly. "Did you know rabbits' teeth never stop growing?"

"So it'll just keep getting bigger and bigger?" Rain asked.

"So majestic," Beatrice cooed.

"Get me closer to it," I said to Bouncer.

Bouncer squinted at me and then turned the steering wheel hard so we were heading directly toward the menacing hare. Bouncer drove around the people and Carrot Con–themed booths. Despite the pandemonium, I couldn't help but notice that one booth was selling cinnamon bunnies and another was selling fake rabbit ears and teeth, and one called Rabbitcadabra was selling bunny-themed magic tricks.

I would have loved for things to be back to normal.

Rabbitcadabra had some cool-looking top hats for sale. But things weren't normal, and Juliet was in serious trouble.

Bouncer drove up as close as he'd dare to get to Big Bun. We stared out the front window. As many people as there were running away, more had their cameras out and were taking pictures of the monster rabbit like he was an attraction for the convention.

"I have a net gun hooked to the back of the truck," Bouncer said.

"What good would that do?" Neil asked. "He's too big."

"What about that fertilizer?" I hollered. "We could spray it at him, and maybe he'll set Juliet down to pick on us."

"Sounds stupid," Rain said. "You should try it."

"That fertilizer has been in there for a while," Bouncer said worriedly. "It'll really smell."

"Even better," I said. "Maybe he'll pass out from the stink."

I quickly scurried over Lady Beatrice and got out of the truck. I ran to the back and climbed up on the side of the metal tank. I found a hose and pulled it around toward the front of the truck. My knees were knocking, and my heart was in my throat, but I had to do something to help Juliet. I turned on the pump and then stood on top of the front of the truck, face-to-face with Big Bun.

Juliet and Big Bun looked down at me. Juliet looked worried, while the rabbit looked curious. He eyed me as I racked my brain for something cool to say.

"Things are about to get stinky!" I yelled.

I pulled open the valve, and the hose shook and then blew fertilizer all over everything. It came out with such force that I couldn't control the hose. I got some on Big Bun, but I also got it all over myself, Juliet, the truck, Bunny Mooners standing around watching . . . basically, everything. It was gritty and green and smelled so horrible I started to gag. The only smell that could have been worse was the Pungent Piles of Putrid Chum that surrounded the city of Sank in *Ocean Blasterzoids*.

I shut the hose down and gagged, which caused me to slip on the grossness that coated the top of the truck. I slid down the front windshield and onto the ground as the Rabbit stomped his feet angrily.

Yep, I'd definitely made him mad.

Big Bun began to thump the street. The ground shook like it was an earthquake. Booths fell over. Trees swayed. Two more windows on the truck exploded. Just when I thought the rabbit was going to crack the island in half, it jumped up from the street and headed north. I got back into the truck, climbing in over Beatrice again.

"That smell!" Beatrice screamed. "I believe I will faint."

"Please do," I said. "Now go, Bouncer! We have to save Juliet!"

Bouncer took a moment to dry heave and then drove. He rolled over the stone path on the other side of Rabbit Road and around a fallen booth called Hare Products.

The sun was just starting to go down, giving the sky a slight tint of yellow. We drove down a dirt road, and I could see the police station up ahead.

"Stop!" I screamed. "We need my uncle. He'll know what to do."

Bouncer skidded to a stop in front of the station.

"Hurry," he ordered.

I ran into the station, dragging Beatrice with me. I knew she was an old mean woman and I was just a kid, but I needed her to get Zeke out. And if comics had taught me anything, it's that sometimes small squids can do remarkable things if they just have the guts to do it. I think she was happy to get out of the truck, where there was more air and less smell.

Melanie was behind the counter, frantically talking into the radio as dozens of calls were coming in with questions about the giant rabbit. Melanie looked like she wouldn't mind dropping everything and having a good cry until she saw Lady Beatrice and froze. Apparently, Carrot Woman had a reputation.

"La . . . Lady Beatrice," she stuttered. "What's that smell?"

"Forget about her," I insisted. "You need to let my uncle out!"

Melanie looked worried. I elbowed Beatrice to remind her that she needed to do her part.

"Fine, fine, fine," she said. "The boy is correct. I will drop the charges, and you can release him."

I believe Melanie just wanted Beatrice and the smell out of the station as quickly as possible because she ran back to the cell and let Zeke out. I was so glad to see him, but there was no time for reunions—Juliet was in trouble.

"We have to go," I told him. "The rabbit has Juliet."

Zeke looked at Beatrice.

"She just got you out," I explained. "So for the moment, pretend she's not completely horrible."

Beatrice sniffed. "The smell, by the way, belongs to your nephew."

We ran to the car and Zeke shoved himself into the backseat with Neil and Rain. I got into the front with Beatrice again.

"Go!" I yelled.

Bouncer took off through the trees and toward the

east end of the island. I tried to quickly fill Zeke in on everything that had happened while scanning the horizon for any sign of Big Bun. But before Zeke could finish asking questions, he gasped.

Out the front window and in the far distance, we could all see a brown mound of fur and ears hopping over the trees with ease. The last time Zeke had seen Big Bun, he had been about the size of a car. Now he was the size of a blimp and leaping so high the whole island shook each time he came down.

"Go faster!" Zeke demanded. "Don't be afraid to hit some trees. He's heading straight to Cottontail Tower."

Bouncer was doing his best to keep up, but the path we were driving on was awful. He had to continually swerve to miss trees and bushes. He also kept bumping over rocks.

"Once we catch the rabbit, how do we stop it?" Zeke yelled while looking at Neil.

"I don't know yet," Neil said.

"Let's worry about getting Juliet first," I insisted. "Then we can deal with Big Bun."

"Of course," Zeke replied.

"We won't stop until Juliet is safe."

"Well," Neil said, "according to my calculations, that might be harder to accomplish than you think. Big Bun isn't getting any smaller."

"We have to try. Juliet is one of the few girls that talk to me," I complained.

"Oh, I've factored all that in," Neil explained. "I just think our chance of success is pretty much nil."

"Nil?" I asked.

"Nothing," he explained.

"No more talking, Neil." Bouncer wasn't in the mood. Like it or not, it was time for us to be heroes.

OCEAN BLASTERZOIDS

SQUID OUT OF WATER

CHAPTER NINETEEN

UNEVEN GROUND

When we got near the cliffs on the east end of the island, Bouncer stopped the truck and pulled up the parking brake. We were on the side of a small sloping hill, looking down at the edge of the island where Cottontail Tower jutted up into the sky. Cottontail Tower was a large, skinny stone that shot upward at least a hundred feet. The locals thought that it resembled a single rabbit ear, but to me that was stretching it. It was shaped more like a rock chimney with a pointed top. From where the truck was parked, we could all see that Big Bun was sitting at the base of Cottontail Tower and holding Juliet. The rabbit was almost half as tall as the stone pillar.

"What's he doing?" I asked. "He won't jump off the cliffs, will he?"

"I don't think so," Zeke said. "That drop would kill him."

"I don't know how to catch a rabbit," I admitted, "but I know what Uli would do."

"Squid tactics," Zeke whispered. "Lead the way, Perry."

We all got out of the truck. Rain's legs were asleep, so getting him out was a chore. We found it was easier to roll him over the seat into the front and then pull him out the bigger front door. We stood him up and waited for him to find his footing. As he regained his land legs, I told the group what we were going to do.

"We're going to split up and move in from five different directions," I said. "We'll each take turns distracting Big Bun. While one of us is yelling at him, the others need to move in closer and freeze. Then like a real squid would do, we'll hold so still that Big Bun won't even notice us. If we do this right, we can get pretty close to him before he reacts. Zeke will move in closest to the right paw, where Juliet is. When he's near enough, he'll grab her feet and wrestle her free."

Bouncer went to the back of the truck. He opened a compartment and pulled something out.

"I've also got this." In his hands was what looked like a long gun with a huge barrel. "It's a net slinger. We use it for netting large herds of bunnies at once. This rabbit's too big, but if there's trouble I could shoot the netting over his head and at least it would distract him for a moment."

"Good," Zeke said.

"Just don't hurt that poor creature," Beatrice insisted.

"I'm not making any promises," Bouncer said. "You put people in danger. I don't want to hurt the rabbit, but I will to save the girl."

I could be wrong, but it looked like once again Beatrice was impressed with Bouncer being so assertive.

"I never wanted anyone to get hurt," she admitted.

"Well then, prove it by helping us," I said.

We all moved slowly to our positions making a large semicircle with Big Bun and Juliet in the middle. The rabbit watched us as we took our spots, but he didn't seem threatened because we weren't very close. Big Bun shifted and put his left paw around Cottontail Tower. Juliet looked at all of us and tried to figure out what our plan was.

We all stayed perfectly still.

I could hear the waves far down below the cliffs and looked at the dimming sky. We needed to act before it got much darker.

"Hey, Big Bun!" I yelled as loud as I could. "Look at me!"

He turned his head and looked at me with his left

eye. As he did, everyone besides me took two slow steps closer to him and froze. I stopped yelling, and Bouncer took a turn.

"Excuse me," he hollered. "You with the massive ears! Look at me, you big rodent!"

Big Bun moved his head and looked at Bouncer. The rest of us moved closer.

"Over here!" Zeke hooted. "I'm talking to you."

Slowly, the semicircle contracted. Big Bun kept turning his head to look at who was screaming. The rabbit seemed confused and almost docile. Neil used his turn to distract the rabbit *and* give us information.

"He might be a little sleepy!" Neil yelled. "He did hop all the way here! He's still a living creature. He can't keep going like this without exhausting himself."

The half circle tightened.

I used my turn to ask, "Are you okay, Juliet?"

The rabbit turned his head to look at me, and I could see Juliet nodding. She kept trying to throw her voice like a ventriloquist, but as I had suspected, she wasn't super-good at it yet. It sounded like the stone pillar was talking, and I could see her lips moving.

"I'd like to get down!" Cottontail Tower seemed to say.

The rabbit looked at the stone pillar.

"We're trying to get you down!" I yelled. Big Bun looked at me again. "Zeke is going to grab you when he can!"

Everyone moved closer.

It was Rain's turn. "I hate this tube! If I ever get out of it, Perry, you're going to pay big-time!"

We were all getting close, and still the rabbit didn't sense the danger. Zeke was almost near enough that he could reach out and grab Juliet's feet, which were dangling as Big Bun held her. It was Beatrice's turn to distract.

"You're spectacular!" she spoke up. "As a rabbit, there is none better!"

We all moved closer. I saw Zeke slowly reaching out to grab Juliet's foot. Unfortunately, as Rain took one step closer, he stumbled. I watched him wobble for a second before he went down. The ground was sloped, so he instantly began to roll toward Big Bun.

Rain screamed, and the rabbit turned his giant body to see what was happening. Spotting the rolling Rain, he lifted his right foot and tried to stomp Rain. But the force of it just managed to pop Rain out of the tube and send him flying into the bushes.

We all froze.

"I'm okay," Rain yelled. I could barely breathe. Zeke was the closest, but it was obvious by the way that Big Bun's whiskers were twitching and his teeth were chattering that he was getting agitated.

It was now or never.

Zeke lunged forward and grabbed Juliet's right foot

as we all screamed to distract the monster bunny.

Big Bun turned his head and hissed while Juliet screamed. Zeke tried to pull her foot, but it was no use. The rabbit screeched and jumped up as high as he could. He came slamming down against the earth.

Juliet kicked and hit the bunny as Big Bun thumped his right foot violently. Zeke tried to grab her again, but the rabbit had other ideas. It jumped up and clung on to the stone pillar with its left paw. His huge rabbit feet scratched the rock structure as it climbed up Cottontail Tower.

Rain screamed from the bushes. "Truck!"

We all turned to see that the fertilizer truck was beginning to roll. Big Bun's thumping had jiggled the brake loose and sent the truck into motion. It rolled down the hill, gaining speed, and headed directly toward the stone pillar.

Juliet saw what was happening and kicked at Big Bun even harder.

We all rushed in as if we had the ability to stop a free-rolling truck, but there was nothing we could do. The truck slammed into the base of Cottontail Tower. There was a tremendous crack as the stones at the bottom broke and the tower began to topple toward the side of the cliff with Big Bun still hanging on.

"Juliet!" I screamed.

Bouncer fired his net gun as the bunny fell. A perfect

shot. Juliet grabbed on to the flying net, and Bouncer yanked her from Big Bun's grip just before the poor animal hit the ground. The top half of the stone pillar struck him on the head with a giant . . .

Carrwhack!

It knocked him out completely. The truck rolled right past his big body and flew over the edge and down into the stones and water below. The sound of the vehicle hitting the rocks was spectacular and unforgettable.

Beatrice looked at the unconscious bunny and began to simultaneously bubble and sob.

I ran to Juliet. She was lying on the ground near the edge in a tangled mess of net.

"Am I alive?" she asked.

"You are."

Rain ran over as well, and the two of us began to untangle her.

"You have arms again," I said to him.

He took a moment to punch me in the shoulder with one of them.

We all gathered around Juliet and struggled with the netting until she was free. Then, as a group, we stood up and turned to look at Big Bun. He was out cold, and large pieces of Cottontail Tower were lying on the ground near him.

"Do you think he's dead?" I asked.

"By my calculations, he could be," Neil said sadly.

Beatrice sobbed and bubbled some more. I was sad to see that such a fantastic creature had bitten the dust, but I was more relieved that Juliet was okay.

But then Big Bun's body began to shake and air escaped from his twitching mouth. I was about to casually scream in terror when I saw that he was starting to shrink. His arms and legs began to convulse and shrivel. His body deflated like a blimp—the air rushing out sounded like the world's loudest, longest whistle! We all plugged our ears and looked on in amazement. The rabbit rocked and thrashed about.

In a matter of minutes, Big Bun was little Bun.

There on the ground was a normal-size rabbit, no different from any others on the island. It looked at all of us, twitched its nose, and then hopped off.

Lady Beatrice held her left hand to her heart while wiping away tears from her eyes with her right one.

"That was . . . incalculable!" Neil exclaimed.

Zeke looked at me and put his hand on my shoulder.

"What a day," he said with a weary smile.

"Yeah," I replied. "I just wish it had been more exciting."

We all turned from the cliffs and headed back.

When we got to town, I was completely surprised. I thought the whole island would be in an uproar about what had happened when Big Bun had stormed through earlier. Instead, everyone seemed excited, and acted as if Big Bun had just been part of a staged Carrot Con experience. Tourists were taking pictures of where the rabbit had knocked things over and hoping it would show up again.

Rain's mom, Flower, hadn't even seen the rabbit. So she was only upset with Rain for not showing up to help. She was also bothered that Zeke hadn't helped either. I'm guessing they explained things to her, but Juliet and I didn't stick around. We got some Carrot Candy, which was just orange cotton candy, and sat on a bench near the face-painting booth.

"Was it weird being carried by a rabbit?" I asked.

"His fur was supersoft."

"That's a relief."

"And it was terrifying."

"I don't know any girl who's as brave as you," I said honestly. "But I don't know many girls, or boys, for that matter."

"I thought I was going to die," she said as her lips turned orange from the carrot candy.

"I'm glad you didn't."

"Me, too."

Juliet smiled. I wondered if I should kiss her, but instead I gave her a thumbs-up. It was almost as awkward as if I had tried to kiss her.

CHAPTER TWENTY
CARROT CON

Two bad things happened the next day. First, Beatrice and Neil didn't get in any trouble for all the mess they had made. Her nephew, Rolly, refused to lock her up or punish her in any way.

"She scares me," he had said.

I couldn't argue with that. So the bubbling lady and Neil had returned to her home to live another day. I guess she was impressed with all that Bouncer had done, because she had hired him back on at twice his pay.

The second bad thing to happen was that Juliet didn't win Junior Miss Carrot. To make things worse, some girl who was allergic to fur and played the harmonica won.

Where is the justice in the world?

Lots of tourists wondered if the giant rabbit would show up again, but it didn't. Everyone was convinced that it was all a huge promotion show for Carrot Con. The public wanted it to come back so they could take more pictures or ride on it like Juliet had.

We all took turns helping Flower sell smoothies from her booth until it was time for us to have our panel presentation at four. The event was held in the Angora Room of the Bunny Hotel. Me, Juliet, Zeke, and Rain sat behind a big table at the front and answered questions about the time we had saved the island from purple carrots and mutant bunnies. There were a lot of good questions, but also a few dumb ones.

"Do you like bunnies?" a woman with a big forehead and sundress asked all of us.

Zeke answered, "Sure."

Juliet said, "Yes."

Rain answered, "Why not?"

And me? I had to think about it. I was more of an under-ocean fan than an aboveground groupie. I wanted to have tentacles and fins and fight newts along with Admiral Uli and my uncle. But even though bunnies needed oxygen and they don't hate newts, they had still been the source of some important times for me.

"So, do you like bunnies, Perry?" the woman asked again.

"They're probably my fourth-favorite animal," I answered.

After the panel was over, I took a few minutes to slip away from everyone and call my dad. I had meant to phone home earlier in the day, but Carrot Con had been very distracting.

"Perry," he said with excitement. "I was just thinking of you. Of course, I always am. I could be wrong, but I don't think you called me yesterday."

"Sorry, it was kind of a busy day."

"I understand. I had to run to the store twice. Once to get cereal and the second time to get the milk. So, tell me, how's the Root Festival?"

"So far, Carrot Con has been great."

I told my dad about the Con and everything that was happening there. I wanted to tell him about Big Bun, but I figured I would wait until I was back home to do that. I didn't want him to worry. Besides, I had plenty of things to fill him in on—what people thought of my hair, the Sharky-Barkys Zeke had given me, my thumbs-up to Juliet, and the questions I'd answered at the panel.

"You're like a plant," he told me. "A plant that is growing and acquiring new leaves with each experience."

"I guess so. I should probably go," I informed him. "They're about to start the Carrot Color Battle. Locals, Bunny Mooners, tourists, everyone is going to throw

183

color bombs at each other."

"Sounds messy," he said. "But I checked the weather for your area, and it looks like it's favorable battle weather. How about you call me again tomorrow and let me know how it went?"

"For sure."

"And, Perry . . ." My dad stopped talking to sniff. "Don't eat any bad wheat."

"I won't eat any wheat at all, Dad."

I hung up the phone and went back to join my friends. The Carrot Color Battle was held in the mall parking lot, where there were tables set up with what looked like millions of orange-colored balls.

We all threw colored balls at each other until everyone involved was orange from head to toe. After it was over, the Carrot Con committee handed out green paper hats for us to wear so we'd look like carrots. I looked at my friends and uncle and smiled. Normally, I hated carrots, but today at least, they looked okay.

"Hey," Zeke said. "We should go swimming in the water pools near Whisker Cliffs to wash off."

Juliet, Rain, and I agreed with him.

We all ran to the falls and swam until the water was good and orange.

OCEAN BLASTERZOIDS
SQUID OUT OF WATER

To be continued...

ABOUT THE AUTHOR

Obert Skye is what some people call an author. Other people might call him an award-winning author with close to thirty books under his belt. Sure, that's a weird place for him to keep his books, but he's run out of shelf space. *Mutant Bunny Island* is inspired by his love for mutants, bunnies, and islands. Three things he thinks the world needs more of. Obert has five kids and a wife and lives in a warm place. Find out more about him at obertskye.com.

ABOUT THE ARTIST

Eduardo Vieira is a freelance character designer and illustrator, trying to find his place in this big world through art. When he's not drawing (which is almost all the time), he likes eating pizza, playing Street Fighter, and having Netflix marathons.

Eduardo currently lives in São Paulo, Brazil, with his girlfriend and their amazing cat.

MORE BOOKS IN THE MUTANT BUNNY ISLAND SERIES!

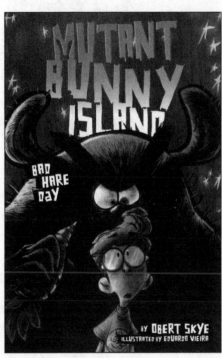

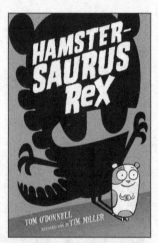